Mouth of God, Light of Infinity

Wassim Elhouar

ISBN: 0989232700
ISBN-13: 978-0-9892327-0-8

Mouth of God, Light of Infinity

Words by
Wassim Elhouar

Words edited by
Albert J. Ballard
&
Maxwell J. Sowell

Artwork by
Joshua Kovarik

Cover designed by
Seth Kasky

For Afif

STORIES

<u>Reel</u>

It happens once a month or so. The town liars are rounded up and forced into the square where everyone can see them. It's not the same people each time. There's a new group each month, and no person is ever taken twice.

This started when I was younger. Things were rotten and not getting better. I've never believed that people are born bad or anything, but I dunno, somewhere down the road we all decided that things like honesty and civility weren't important. We could still smile and make small talk with each other, but you knew nobody meant anything. It elevated as time went on, spreading into business affairs and starting to seriously affect the local economy.

It didn't matter. Nearly everywhere you looked you could see the same smug expression on people's faces. They could bullshit you and get away with it. Consequences are for the broken.

A few years ago, during our last election, we got a new mayor. He was a burly mutherfucker, physically imposing and every bit the straight-talker the people who voted for him weren't. There wasn't much money around. He promised us a way out. Economy through honesty, he said.

It started pretty simply. You'd see posters in stores and on the street, commercials on T.V. You'd hear radio announcers instructing the townsfolk how to behave with one another. It was unavoidable, a full-on media blitz trying to change people's behavior.

It didn't work. Some people put in an honest-to-God effort but fell back into their old ways. The mayor himself never seemed convinced the plan would work. Too soft, he said.

So he went and made lying an outright crime. We were confused when the news broke. Most people just laughed and carried on with themselves. But he got us, and he got us good. Whatever money was left was put towards wiring the whole damn place up and creating some sort of undercover police force, tasked with blending in with everyone else and eavesdropping on them.

Nobody knew about it for the first several weeks or so. One day a lot of us received letters in the mail warning that we'd been caught lying or being deceptive. Consequences will be severe, the letters said.

We found out how severe days later. Word got out that something was happening in the town square. When I got there I saw a big crowd gathered. And I saw gallows. There wasn't a noose in sight but there were hooks. Ten hooks.

We watched as guards marched out ten people, each one convicted of telling some sort of serious lie. One by one they stepped forward. Tongues out, the guards said. Then they hooked them. And they hung them.

It takes only seconds for a tongue to get ripped out. Some die from the shock right there and then. Some bleed to death. Some off themselves not too long after. Those who survive are rarely seen in public. The dead are burned in piles.

The screams alone were enough to scare most people. The town got quieter as a whole, but I gotta say, business did start falling back into place as more people cleaned up their acts. Of course there have been idiots who thought they could get away with it, and there have been people too stupid to know better. They've been slowly disappearing but there are still some around.

I know a few people personally who were on the wrong end of the law. Just last month they got this girl I went to school with. She spent three months talking and flirting some poor bastard up, then at the end of it she told him she never cared to begin with. Broke his heart so much he almost didn't make it to her hanging. But he did, and he smiled while it happened. Wasn't a clean rip. Girl shook and thrashed so much that only part of her tongue came off. She landed on her head, dented her skull. Still alive, I hear, eating through a tube and weeping her eyes out every day.

They've got six lined up for later this month. Same fate as all the others. We've already lost a couple hundred over the years, not to mention all the crippled and demented souls.

Civic virtue through brutality. It works, but it makes you wonder how long this sort of thing will go on.

Maybe till we're all gone.

Mein

She told me she'd never seen the ocean. Considering how close we live to the coast I thought it was a real shame. I told her I could take her someday. She told me the ocean didn't want her.

She started working at my office five months ago. Her name was Violet. She had just moved into the area from the Midwest, said she'd always wanted to get out here. I remember asking her why this city. She said it was fate.

Twenty-seven years old, she said. Unmarried, not looking and trying to live life to the fullest. She wanted to experience something new, because what is life if you stay in the same place all your years? Her plan was to work here for a little bit and then go somewhere else, maybe overseas. I admired that. I've been here all my life and never had the money to travel. To see someone ambitious at a relatively young age was refreshing. It was attractive.

My life growing up was mediocre. My father was a carpenter and my mother was a secretary. I had no siblings, though it wasn't for a lack of trying. My father always spoke of wanting another daughter, as did my mother. I suppose someone had a different idea, because my parents had me and that was it. Was my mother infertile? We weren't sure. Either she was and I was a miracle or she had me and then her body decided it was enough.

We lived in a small home a few blocks away from my elementary school. My parents worked while I was at school, so I was picked up each day by our neighbor, Mrs. Agnew. She was a nice woman, elderly and widowed. She helped with my homework and let me watch Bonanza with her. Sometimes she showed me pictures of her grandchildren and told stories about them. Mrs. Agnew took care of me for several years before she passed away. I remember the day well. I was the one who found her. She told me she was going to lay down because she felt a little tired. I was sitting in the living room doing school work.

An hour or two came and went before I realized she was still in her room. It was unusual because I remember her saying she never slept much. I walked into her room and saw her lying on her bed. My first thought was to wake her up, but when I came closer I noticed she was not breathing. I watched her for a few minutes to see if she would stir. Not a twitch. I left her and went back to my work. When my parents came to pick me up I opened the door and let them in. They called out to thank her. When she didn't answer they looked for her. They walked into the kitchen, then the restroom and finally her bedroom. My mother shrieked. My father called for the police. When they arrived they asked if I knew Mrs. Agnew had died. I said no. Then they took her away in the ambulance. My parents and I went home. I was eight.

The following years brought multiple babysitters. Most were like our late neighbor, old and alone. But when I was eleven my parents found a young woman in her twenties, studying at a local college and trying to make some extra money. Her name was Helen. Blonde and voluptuous. The moment I saw her I knew I wanted her.

I always behaved around Helen. I did my work when she asked and went to bed when I was supposed to. If there was cleaning to be done I helped her. And if her favorite program was on I would sit next to her and we would watch together.

Helen loved me too. She was always smiling and laughing, referring to me as her "little monster" and bragging to her friends that I was so much fun. How distraught I was when I found out she was seeing someone. His name was Carl, and he went to school with her. I never met him, but in the depths of my imagination I like to think that he was a no-good, hideous, putrid-smelling human being and she had made a mistake in seeing him. They wouldn't last very long, and soon she would be mine again.

Each day grew worse. Though Helen didn't make any drastic changes she spoke of Carl more and more. Carl is taking me to a ball game! or Carl bought me a necklace! is all I heard. If there was a way to get rid of the wretched man without hurting Helen I would have done it in a heartbeat.

She continued to babysit me for another year, during which she graduated from college and announced to the family that she and Carl were engaged and moving to Wyoming in the summer. The utter disgust I felt! I vividly remember the day she came to bid my family and I goodbye. I stood there crying, tears running down my face. I felt pathetic and angry. Helen was being taken away from me. She was happy. I was nothing.

I have not seen or heard from her since. After she left, my mother quit her job so she could spend more time with me. My father continued to work. I finished middle school, then high school, and then entered university. The years since then aren't worth mentioning. I was a sullen teenager and then became a sullen university student. I made new friends during my college stay but Helen was always in the back of my mind. No other women interested me.

My mother passed away during my graduating year at university. My father was devastated in the most restricted of ways. I wasn't sure what to feel. I barely knew her.

I lived with my father for a year after graduation. I thought it would be best to support him, as our nearest family members lived some distance away. We were not close, but having someone in the house helped him. I took care of him while I searched for a job. I worked at a small deli while I looked. My father retired as arthritis invaded his fingers. My earnings along with what little savings he had got us by.

He spent his time inside, usually sitting in his chair. He would read the newspaper and then listen to talk radio. Sometimes he would go outside and walk. He asked me every once in a while, Do you miss your mother? And I would tell him I hadn't really thought about her. I was occupied with work and trying to find a meaningful job. Besides, there was no room for my mother in my memories. All I had, and all I needed, was Helen. I don't know why my father kept asking me the same question when I kept giving him the same answer. A scowl always followed.

We got to a point where my money could no longer sustain us both. My father needed more care and attention with each passing week. I made the decision to put him in a home. It helped him because there would be someone able to help him at any time. It helped me because I would not have to deal with the stress of work and caring for him. I could be alone.

I found a better job when I was about 24. An accountant at a local company. I was excited. It meant I was one step closer to independence. It meant I could find my own house soon. It meant new people and new experiences.

I started the following month. I had a tidy little desk and my own nameplate. I had a telephone and a typewriter. The pay was good, certainly enough for me to move out of my parents' home after several months. I came to work on time every day and stayed later than most. I remember feeling happy, the happiest I had felt in a long time. I made some friends. This was strange because for the first time I had something to do other than care for my father.

This was my life for the next twenty-three years. I worked, I went home, and sometimes I went out. I kept the same small group of friends. My romantic life was non-existent. Heaven knows I tried. I became acquainted with a few women through my friends. I even tried to get to know some of the workers. But nothing happened. Some were taken. Most were not interested. Helen was a fading memory at this point, but her ghost lingered in the back of my mind enough that I could never forget her.

Loneliness is an awful feeling. Growing up with no siblings had its share of perks, namely the attention, but there was nobody else to play with. I did not have many friends going through school. I had no girlfriends. All I had were my aging parents and myself. I thought things would change once I found a career. They did, in some ways. I was working a good job and had more than enough money for myself. I had new friends and plans on the weekends. But when I went home it was just myself. Sometimes I lay in bed for hours on end and stared at the ceiling. It would have been wonderful to have someone to come home to and cook for. Someone to lay with me. Someone who would never leave me. That is what I wanted.

Things changed when I saw Violet walk into the office for the first time. Blonde and voluptuous. Some strange and great feeling ran down my body. The moment I saw her I knew I wanted her. And nothing would stop me this time.

Violet was one of our new secretaries. I was friends with one of them already, so being introduced would not be a problem. Her desk would not be very far from mine. I made it a priority to meet her as soon as I could.

At first I admired her from afar. I would see her work. See her smile. See her laugh. I soon asked another secretary if she would introduce me, and she said yes. That day I made sure I looked my best. I was cheerful and upbeat, eager to make the best first impression possible.

Twenty-seven years old, she said, straight out of a city in Iowa. She was unmarried. Single, in fact. She said she moved because she wanted a change of scenery. Life was getting dull and she wanted to shake it up a bit. I asked her why she chose our city. Violet said it was fate. She was weighing her options one day when it just popped into her head. And it was decided.

She said she did not plan to stay for very long. She wanted to work for maybe two or three years and then go somewhere else. Europe weighed heavily on her mind, as she had heard about opportunities to teach English in schools.

It would be incredible to experience the history and culture, she said. I hope I can find a way over there.

We talked about her hobbies. She liked to jog and she liked to read. She liked to see movies and visit museums. I asked her if she had any interest in going to the beach. She told me she'd never seen the ocean and hadn't bothered to since moving out here. I told her there isn't a better sight than a sunrise at the beach. Violet said the water didn't want her.

I went home that night deeply enamored. There was a young, gorgeous, ambitious woman that worked a few steps away from me. She could be mine. And I would make her so.

Over the following weeks I spoke to her more. I would pass by her desk and say a friendly good morning, or maybe stop for a little chat. Sometimes we'd talk during lunch or after work. She soon started coming out with my friends and me. We'd go out to eat and go out for drinks. Sometimes we went to art galleries or plays. No matter what we did Violet was enthused. It was contagious. I can't remember being happier.

It struck me one night, after I had come home from a bar, that Violet was no ordinary young woman. She was Helen reincarnated. Some spiritual force had put her here for me, to make amends for taking Helen away when I was younger. Violet was mine.

As we became friendlier I tried to make my intentions clearer. I flirted with her and stood close to her. I couldn't tell how she felt. She was always smiling and in a good mood. She clearly wasn't rejecting me, but did she feel for me as I felt for her? The anticipation made my skin crawl.

I made my move on a Friday. I had a small bouquet of flowers delivered to her desk with a note, saying it said it was from a secret admirer at work. It said to meet at the steakhouse at 7 that evening.

I arrived at the restaurant ten minutes early and waited in the lobby. I wore my best clothes. I tried to imagine how Violet would react. I was sure she would be happy. And I would be happy. We would be happy together.

I looked at my watch. Seven came. I did not see her. A few minutes passed. I still did not see her. I became anxious. I did not consider the possibility that she may not even come.

7:10.

7:15.

I waited like a fool. My heart sank. This was a mistake, I thought. I should have tried something else. Maybe I should have kept to myself. Anything that would have prevented this embarrassment.

Then she walked in. She looked around the lobby for a moment and then spotted me. I tried to relax as she walked over.

Hello, she said, are you here meeting someone too?

Yes, I said, I guess you could say that.

I got some flowers and a mysterious note at work saying to meet here. I think they might be from James. He's been awful friendly to me lately.

I could not keep from grinning.

I sent them, I said.

Violet kept smiling. It was clear she was shocked.

Oh, she said. Did you mean them as a gift?

That's one way to look at it, I said.

I think she wanted to leave, but she did not move. She looked around the lobby for a few seconds and then said she may as well stay since she had bothered to dress up and come out. We were seated in a small booth near the back of the restaurant.

Dinner was awkward. Yes, we made polite conversation, and no, there weren't any long stretches of silence. It was her aura and body language. The way she looked at her food. The way her eyes wandered to other tables while I was speaking. She was nervous. I suggested going for a drink afterwards. She declined. I paid the bill. We exchanged a quick good night and went our separate ways.

I went home feeling, as I had in my youth with Helen, angry and humiliated. I lay in bed and relived the evening over and over again in my head. Each time my heart fell further into the deepest throes of pity.

Work was not the same after our dinner. Violet no longer had any interest in small talk. Whenever I passed by her desk she would look down at her work or start speaking with someone else. As this went on I stopped blaming myself and began to direct my resentment towards her. I stopped seeing a lovely young woman and started seeing her for what she truly was. A care-free, snobbish little girl with no regard for others' feelings. She couldn't even apologize to me.

Some of the girls from work were going out for drinks on a Saturday in early February. I learned Violet would be there. By this time I had moved past my animosity and found myself feeling sorry for the girl. I asked if I could come with them. The girls said yes.

It was a great time. Everyone was lively and laughing, telling funny stories, singing karaoke. Everyone was drunk. I stayed sober. The night began to wear on and some of the ladies had to go home. Soon it was myself, Violet and the other secretary. Both had come in a cab and were thinking about leaving. I offered them a ride.

We continued to talk on the way home. I dropped off the other girl and started for my place. Violet was in the back seat. She was trying to tell me about a silly incident that happened at her previous job. She didn't realize what was happening until I pulled into my neighborhood.

Where are we, she said.

I need to take care of something at home, I said. You can come in, I won't be long.

Violet followed me in. I turned on the lights, locked the door and went to my room. I had to calm myself for a moment. Here she was. Finally alone with me. I was not going to waste the opportunity.

I walked back out to the living room. She sat on my couch. I sat down next to her and gazed into her eyes. I touched her thigh.

She grabbed my hand and removed it. I caressed her back.

Why would you do that, I said.

Violet said she'd made it very clear how she felt. She pushed my hand away and tried to run to the door. I grabbed her arm and pulled her back. Nothing would stop me this time.

You got away from me once, I said, but you won't now.

I pulled her towards me. She smelled of alcohol and sweet perfume. I forced my lips on hers. Her eyes flew open with absolute distress.

She smacked me.

I smacked her harder.

She fell onto the couch. I walked to my closet and grabbed a small piece of rope. When I returned she was still on her face, crying quietly. I brought over one of the chairs from my dining table and ordered her to sit. No response. I waited for a minute. I grew impatient. I grabbed her arm and dragged her up and into the chair. Then I tied her up.

She was a mess of tears and runny make-up. Snot ran down from her nose. She was whimpering. I reached out and ran my fingers down her cheek. Then I brushed them up and down her throat. I smiled as I looked at her.

Tell me you love me, I said.

No reply.

I gripped her neck. Violet, I said, tell me you love me.

No reply. I choked her a little harder.

It's not so hard dear, I said. Repeat after me. I love you.

Hyeluvyoo, she managed to say.

And I need you.

Hyeneedyoo.

I paused for a moment, keeping my grip firm. I saw panic in her eyes. She searched for God in mine. Her pulse quickened. I think she knew what was coming.

Now give me what I want, I said. Her sobbing grew louder. I leaned over and kissed her. I kissed her lips. I kissed her cheeks. I kissed her neck. I tasted the salt from her tears. I breathed in her wonderful aroma.

I stood up and walked to the kitchen. I came back with a plastic bag. I told Violet to close her eyes. She stared at me.

Close your eyes, I said.

But they stayed open.

I was not in the mood for games. I smacked her several times and screamed at her to close her eyes. When she finally did I took a deep breath.

Be still, young flower, I said.

I put the bag over her head and fastened it. Then I walked to my room and waited. I heard her scream. She knocked herself over in the chair and thrashed about. I heard the life peter out of her.

I waited a little while longer to be safe. It was nearly two in the morning when I walked back out to the living room. I found her on the ground, cold and lifeless. I removed the bag from her head, untied her and picked her up. Her eyes were closed. Her mouth was half open. I went to the bathroom and got a damp towel. I wiped her face clean.

She was beautiful again. I smiled.

I lifted her from the chair onto my shoulder. I carried her into my room. I changed into my nightgown and helped her change too. She wanted to sleep on the right side of the bed. I tucked her in, turned the lights off and kissed her good night. I wrapped my arms around her and we fell asleep.

Violet and I slept in the next morning. I woke up and found her facing me. I kissed her on the cheek and said good morning. We got up and went to the kitchen to make brunch. After we ate we sat in the living room to watch television. I held her hand and snuck a glance every so often. We finished watching and cleaned around the house. Then we sat down for some afternoon reading. We made dinner afterwards. I talked to her as we ate. She said she was happy I came into her life. I told her I was happy too, because it meant I would no longer be lonely. We went to bed as we did the previous night, embracing each other.

I called into work sick on Monday. I wanted to spend more time with Violet. The day brought more of the same. I couldn't help but notice how pale she looked. She no longer smelled sweet either. She smelled rather sour.

I went back to work on Tuesday. I had left Violet alone at home, which worried me because I wasn't sure she could take care of herself. I walked into the office and greeted everyone as normal. One of the girls we had gone out with over the weekend said nobody had heard from Violet since. When she was gone on Monday they thought she may have been sick, though it was strange she did not return any of the company's phone calls. By mid-day Tuesday they were worried. They asked me if I had seen her. I said no, I took her home on Saturday, hadn't heard a peep from her since.

The rest of the day was filled with tension and anxiety. I was not sure what to do with Violet, who was surely going to get me in trouble. I finished my work and left as soon as I could. Violet was in the living room when I walked in, reading Jane Austen. It was one of her favorites. I told her she could not stay past tonight. She did not reply. I gave her a small kiss and changed into a t-shirt and some jeans. Then I prepared dinner.

I figured out what I'd do as we washed the dishes. But I didn't tell her. I waited until just after midnight, when I told her we were going for a ride. I helped her out of the house and into the car. Then I drove for the bridge.

I tried to find somewhere closed off, somewhere we wouldn't be easily spotted. I parked to the side and pulled Violet out. We looked over the railing, down at the water. It was dark and calm. She looked scared. I told her she would be ok.

I gave her one last kiss. Then I pushed her over the rail and into the water. I watched her sink to the bottom. Then I went home.

My coworkers called the police the next day. I was among those questioned, as I was the last to see her alive.

I told them she'd never seen the ocean, and I thought that was a shame.

Drive

The young man stood on his front porch. It was hot outside. Almost unbearably hot. He held prayer beads in one hand. Not because he was religious, but because he liked the tranquility they brought. In his other hand was his cell phone.

He looked at the time. He was waiting for his friend. She was late.

Nine minutes and counting.

He looked towards the end of the street. No sight of her. He thought about calling. Then he figured she'd be there soon, so he didn't. He walked inside and sat on a chair. He looked at the table next to him. A few magazines were scattered across it. One in particular advertised beautiful vistas and starry nights. He thought it might be a nice place to visit.

He glanced at the time again.

He sighed. The girl had told him she was never late. Except today, apparently.

They had met at a local record shop. She was eyeing the copy of John Coltrane's My Favorite Things he was holding. He put it down. She asked if he was going to buy it. He said no.

You like Coltrane? he said.

Yes, I do, she said.

They talked about jazz and they talked about other music. Her name was Alicia. She had just graduated university but was unable to find work. He was still a student.

After discovering their shared interest in independent films he asked her if she'd be interested in going out sometime.

Yes, she said, that would be great.

They exchanged numbers and agreed to meet soon.

I'm mostly free, she said. Unemployed twenty-two-year-olds don't have much to do.

I bet, he said.

He had texted her the previous night.

Would you like to go driving tomorrow?

Yes.

Cool. Do you mind if you drive?

I guess not.

I can give you gas money.

Ok. What time?

5:30, he said.

That's fine, she said.

It was now 5:48. He was still waiting. He walked back to the porch. There was a small red car coming his way. It stopped in front of him. Alicia got out. She looked nervous.

Sorry, she said. I accidentally took a nap.

No problem, he said.

They got in the car. She started driving out of the neighborhood.

Where are we going, she said.

I don't know. Somewhere far away. I don't care where, just far.

He took out a twenty and put it in one of the cup holders.

That's for gas, he said.

They left the neighborhood. He sat and stared out the window. She looked straight ahead as she drove. It was like this for a few miles. Alicia looked at him. He hadn't moved.

So how's your day been, she said.

Uncle hung himself this morning.

...I. Well. Shit. I'm sorry to hear that.

He said nothing.

Why are you here then?

Cause I sure as hell don't wanna be over there.

Over there being?

My grandmother's house. That's where they found him.

Don't you think you should at least be there for support?

No, he said. I don't think so.

Why?

Just drive.

He continued to gaze out the window. They drove past restaurants and grocery stores, doctors' offices and florists. They drove through the town square, which Alicia found to be the most beautiful part of the city. Especially in the summer. Every Saturday evening part of the square was closed to traffic and local musicians would perform. There was a blues group playing in four days. She didn't like the blues.

They started driving out of the city. The highway was mostly empty and surrounded by nothing but fields. She peeked at him. He was looking at the car ceiling.

Do you mind if I crack the window, he said.

I've got the AC on.

He opened it anyway. She was tempted to say something but kept her mouth shut. They reached a small town.

I don't even feel bad.

I'm sorry?

I said I don't feel bad, he said. About what happened today.

Your uncle?

Yeah. Him.

Why?

Cause the way I see it - hey, can you pull over here?

He pointed at a gas station up ahead.

Sure, said Alicia.

She parked the car.

I'll be back, need to use the bathroom, he said.

He got out and walked in. She decided to go in too. He turned around and looked at her.

You're not gonna follow me to the toilet are you?

No, I'm getting a drink.

He nodded and made for the restroom. Alicia picked up a bottle of iced tea and then looked at the candy and chocolate bars. She eyed a Twix bar, but thought she might want M&Ms instead. She glanced towards the bathroom door. He was just stepping out. He walked over to her.

Are you ready to go, he said.

Just about.

Actually, gimme a sec, I wanna grab something to eat too.

He went to the next aisle and picked up a bag of chips. They paid and left.

Do you think we should start driving back towards the city? said Alicia. We're getting pretty far away.

I think we should drive a little more, he said.

She drove. He ate his chips. Sometimes she sipped her iced tea.

You haven't told me why you don't feel bad, said Alicia.

Yeah.

Well?

He did it to himself. That's why. And I don't mean the stunt he pulled this morning. Everything leading up to it, it was all him. Lost his family, lost damn near all his money.

Sounds rough.

Yeah, maybe I'd care if it was bad luck or some horseshit like that. But it wasn't.

What was it then?

He looked at her.

I'm not gonna sit here and give you a full rundown on my relatives' problems, he said. I'll tell you this though: nothing good comes out of messing around with other women and throwing other peoples' money around.

Alicia didn't look at him.

I still think you could at least show some sympathy, she said. Or be there for your family members.

I don't wanna be there. Everyone's probably still hysterical and bawling their eyes out. Not my thing.

Another stretch of silence. They were very far from home now. Alicia guessed they were fifty or sixty miles out. She wanted to turn back but was afraid of upsetting him. His eyes were fixed on his phone. She wished she would have stayed home.

And you know what's funny? MCA died -

Who's MCA?

One-third of the Beastie Boys, he said. Died last month. And I shed a few tears. I still think about it. Uncle dies? Barely knew him, don't care. I picture some poor bastard mustering up every excuse he can think of and then saying Fuck it, someone's out to get me, life's unfair, I'm done.

You don't think maybe he did it because he realized it was all his doing? said Alicia.

Maybe. I doubt it. Someone with any sense at all would try to fix it, don't you think?

People don't always act logically.

No wonder he's chillin' at the morgue right now with a goddamned crushed esophagus.

He went back to his phone. Alicia fought the urge to throw him out of the car and drive home. She thought about it. Then she took the next exit.

I'm going back, she said.

Why?

Because we've been driving for two hours and I have no idea where we are.

Isn't that the thrill though?

Do you do this often?

Used to. Me and an old friend used to drive nowhere, park the car and sit outside and talk, he said.

Where's your friend now?

Dunno. Haven't talked in a while.

I see.

He looked out the window. You know, he said, I think one of my dad's friends lives somewhere out this way.

That's nice, said Alicia.

He leaned his chair back. She drove and didn't want to say anything to him.

Wanna hear how they found him?

Silence.

Ok. Well. One of my cousins - not one of his kids - was gonna go run errands with him.

I didn't say I wanted to hear it.

My uncle said he'd be at my grandma's house. Cousin finds the front door unlocked, walks in, calls out for him. Doesn't get an answer.

I don't want to hear this.

So he looks around the place. First the kitchen, then the basement, then he walks upstairs. And in my grandma's room, what's he find?

Stop.

There's the man, hanging by his own belt. Legs still had a bit of kick in them. He wriggled a bit. Then he let out one last –

Alicia slammed on the brakes.

What the hell are you doing?

I swear, I am this close to booting you out and making you walk home.

She glared at him. He didn't give a damn.

He let out one last bitch breath and that was it, he said. Gone. Shit his khakis in the process.

She pulled over to the side of the road and got out. He stayed inside. After a few minutes he turned around and saw her standing behind the car. She was facing away from him. He pulled his phone out and checked the news.

Alicia stood with her arms crossed. She cried for a couple of minutes and sniffled for a few more. She looked back at the car. He didn't seem the least bit concerned. She wiped her face with her shirt and went back.

Are you better now, he said.

She started the car.

I'm really not sure why you had to be that dramatic.

Her eyes were still moist.

Are you mad at me?

I thought we were gonna go on this drive and talk about music and stuff, not how your uncle offed himself, she said. I thought you'd be a lot more pleasant than this.

Funny how people always let you down, isn't it?

Fuck off.

He grimaced at her. Then his eyes shifted to the window.

And in case you were curious, Alicia said, my day was very enjoyable until I picked you up. I woke up early, I exercised, I finished reading a book and I relaxed a little. My girlfriends asked if I wanted to hang out with them and I said, No, I'm going out with a guy who likes the same stuff I like and seems pretty neat.

He was silent.

Then it turns out he's some insensitive asshole.

It happens, he said.

That was the end of any conversation between them for the next twenty minutes. He shut his eyes. She drove. She couldn't wait to drop him off at his house and never have to see him again. She wondered what he did in his spare time.

Probably one of those guys that stays at home on the weekend and picks fights on the internet, she thought.

The sun was setting. Alicia turned her headlights on. He was still asleep. Or maybe just quiet with his eyes closed. She liked him better this way.

The exit for their city was in a couple of miles. She drove a little faster and hoped he wouldn't wake up.

She hoped too soon.

If you could pick only five bands to listen to for the rest of your life, what would they be?

She took the exit.

You wanted to talk about music, come on. It couldn't be any worse than awkward silence while you drive in anger.

I'm not angry, she said.

Frustration.

She didn't want to talk to him. She didn't want to do much of anything.

I like The Stone Roses. Modest Mouse. Spoon. Belle & Sebastian. Röyksopp might be my all-time favorite.

Those are good choices, he said.

Thanks.

That was it for the rest of the drive. He didn't say another word. Just ahead was the city. She was grateful.

Soon they came across the familiar. They drove through the town square. They drove past restaurants and grocery stores, doctor's offices and florists. Then they got to his neighborhood. She turned onto his street and pulled up to his house.

This was interesting, he said.

He unbuckled his seat belt and opened the door. He stepped out.

I'm sorry again about your uncle, said Alicia. But she didn't look at him.

He shut the door and walked away.

She drove home.

The Subject Was Faggots

The kid was new and nobody knew him.

He'd just transferred from another city a couple of weeks before. Decent student, monster of a basketball player. Helped lead his old school to second in his state. There were rumors he was going to be the first sophomore on the varsity team in five years.

The school paper wanted an interview with him. One of those get to know the new guy features. So he found himself in a bathroom one Thursday afternoon, looking in the mirror and reassuring himself that he wasn't gonna fuck it all up. Then he walked to the library.

When he entered there was a girl waiting for him at one of the tables.

Hey there, she said.

Hey.

How's it going?

Pretty good, pretty good, he said as he sat across from her.

Ready to get this interview done?

Yeah.

The girl had a notebook and a tape recorder sitting on the table.

Is it ok with you if I record this? Helps me avoid mistakes later.

Doesn't bother me, he said.

Great, she said.

She unwrapped a fresh cassette and put it in the machine. Then she pressed record.

Can you give me your full name please.

Ray Hamilton.

Thank you. So tell me, how're you liking our school so far?

It's bigger than my old one but I'm getting used to it. Some cool people around here. Excited to play basketball.

Yeah, tell me more about that. Did the coaches approach you, did you go to a tryout, what happened?

Combination of both really, he said. Someone heard about me through the grapevine, passed it on to the coaches. They asked me to come shoot around with some guys from the team. So I did, and they liked what they saw.

They must have, I hear you might make varsity, said the girl. Does that intimidate you at all?

I mean, not really. I'm grateful to play and I'll give my best to whatever team I end up on. Junior-varsity, varsity, doesn't matter. I wanna work hard and win.

I bet the coaches like hearing that, she said.

Ray smiled.

Enough about basketball, she said, tell me about your move here. What prompted that?

Nothing much to that, you know, my dad found a new job here, we decided we wanted a change of scenery, so we up and moved.

Has it been tough for you to adjust? I remember when I was like seven years old and my family moved here, I had to make new friends and get used to a new school. It felt overwhelming.

A little bit. I've talked to people from my classes, sat with them at lunch. It's one of those things that'll happen as time passes.

She flipped to a new page in her notebook.

How about hobbies, she said, what are you into?

Music. I've got my dad's old records in my room, stuff like Smokey Robinson and Anita Baker. I've got more contemporary stuff too. When I'm in my room, relaxing or doing homework or something, I just put on an album and get into my zone.

Any favorites from this year?

Well I liked *De La Soul is Dead* a lot. *Death Certificate* and *Organized Konfusion* - those came out a few days ago. Great albums, both of them, but I think my favorite this year is Gang Starr's *Step in the Arena*.

I've never heard of any of those, said the girl.

What do you listen to? said Ray.

A lot of alternative stuff, bands like Ween, Smashing Pumpkins, Fugazi.

I can't say I've heard of any of them either.

The interview came out the following Friday, November 8th. Ray took two copies of the paper that day, one for himself and one for his father. Mr. Hamilton read it during dinner.

You would mention my records and not say a thing about me, he said.

Ray laughed.

If I get another interview I'll make sure half of it is devoted just to you, he said.

Like that'll happen.

Just wait and see, pops.

They ate for a few minutes.

Now how come I haven't met any of these friends of yours yet, said Mr. Hamilton. I've heard you mention a couple of names but I haven't seen any faces.

I haven't hung out with anyone that much outside of school, said Ray. Sometimes I hit the arcade with a couple of guys from the team.

Well it'd sure be nice to meet them.

You can come to one of my games, pops.

Ray had, in fact, been hanging out quite a bit with someone. His name was Craig. He was the varsity team's starting center. Tall, good-looking guy. They started talking one day after practice when someone mentioned the Charlotte Hornets.

I don't even know how they constantly sell out their home games, said Matt, one of the guards.

I don't think they're that bad, said Shaun, one of the forwards.

Yeah, they lost what, fifty-six games last season? Not bad at all.

Nope, said Craig.

What do you think Ray, said Teon, another forward.

I think they've been garbage. But I wouldn't be surprised if they got good in the future.

Don't hold your breath, said Craig.

They stood outside the gym and talked about sports. Craig said he liked baseball and golf more than basketball. Classier sports, he said, but he liked the latter's pace and energy.

I couldn't do golf. Shit's boring, said Ray.

Man, you're something else. You think the Hornets will make the playoffs soon and you hate golf. Lemme guess, you watch *Murder, She Wrote* with your parents every Sunday?

Me and my dad's favorite show.

They laughed.

Alright well listen man, I gotta get going home, said Craig. But here's my number, gimme a call and let's kick it sometime, go shoot hoops at the Y or something. Have a good one.

Craig walked to his bus stop. Ray walked home. He looked at the number on the piece of paper and grinned.

The season started towards the end of November. Ray didn't expect to play much, but he was surprised when he didn't play the first two games. The team scraped by in the first with a home win against a lesser school in the area. They lost the second by fifteen points. Coach wasn't thrilled.

We might have to rotate a few of you guys in the next one, he said after the loss. See what works out.

Ray and Craig talked on the bus ride home.

I'm not sure what went wrong out there. I thought we had a chance to win it, said Ray.

Probably didn't help that we turned the ball over about a hundred times, said Craig.

Twenty-two.

Thanks for counting.

Gotta do something while I'm on the bench.

Craig couldn't help but laugh at him.

So what are you doing this weekend Ray?

Probably homework and helping my dad around the house. Church on Sunday. How about you?

About the same for me. Think you'll be free on Saturday?

Yeah, said Ray, what's up?

If you wanna you can come over and play some Sega with me. We could talk tactics about our next game.

If I even play.

You heard coach tonight, said Craig. He'll be throwing in some fresh faces. Which means you.

Hah, alright.

Ray went to Craig's house on Saturday afternoon. They played video games and they ate pizza. They talked about their game on Thursday. Craig said they needed to up the intensity.

I think as long as we don't try to rush anything we'll do well, said Ray. I saw us make some real garbage plays yesterday, nothing I'd be proud to say I was a part of.

Craig teased him.

You're talking like that now, let's see how you do when you're out on that court. You won't score more than six points.

Bet you I'll get at least ten.

Five bucks.

Deal.

Ray went home early in the evening. He ate dinner with his father and then listened to music in his room. On Sunday he went to church and then studied awhile.

Monday flew by. So did Tuesday. Wednesday too. It was Thursday, the day he was supposed to make his debut, that dragged. He sat in each class and watched the clock tick the minutes away with an unbearable lack of urgency. He made note of this to his friends at lunch.

You think about this too much and you'll put too much pressure on yourself out there, said Teon.

And there's nothing worse than watching the new guy play like shit, said Shakeel, who was due to start that night.

Ray tried to keep his mind off the game for the rest of the afternoon. When school got out he went straight home and took a nap.

The game was at seven. Coach told them to show up at five-thirty. Ray woke up at a quarter-to-five. He prepared his bag. His dad wished him good luck. He left.

Coach laid out the plan in the locker room.

Keep your eyes open, he said. Pass wisely. Don't get caught on the counter-attack. And most importantly, don't get hot-headed.

He announced the starters. Ray was one of them.

The players changed into their jerseys and hit the court to warm up. Ray took some shots. He looked around the court. People were already coming in. Soon it would be a full house. His father would be there too.

Taking it all in? said Craig.

Yeah, said Ray.

I know this is probably a lot bigger than your old school, but trust me, once you get your game going you won't notice shit around you. It'll be just you and the ball.

Anything else?

Yeah. Your five dollars better be ready at the end of the game

.

Coach and the team huddled for one last talk. They riled themselves up and walked onto the court.

Tip-off. Game started.

Ray felt a little out-of-sync with his teammates for most of the first half. Missed an easy lay-up. Tried a three-pointer when it would have been better to pass. A couple of rebounds slipped right out of his fingers. He was benched with a few minutes left.

I think you're trying too hard, said Coach. Your heart's in the right place, just focus on doing your part well.

The game was tied at the half. The team went into the locker room.

I don't know what it is, but some of you guys are playing with no energy at all, said Coach. We're lucky we're not losing, but if you guys don't step it up in the second half we will lose.

They walked back out. Second half started. Ray was still on the bench. He waited. He watched his teammates. He watched his opponents.

He got back in the game seven minutes into the half. He still had no points. He took a deep breath. Then he played.

And he did all right. Nine points, six assists, three rebounds. The team went on a twelve-two run in the final minute and won the game by eight. Coach seemed pleased enough, as did the team. They gathered for a post-game talk and then hit the showers. Ray handed Craig the five dollars after they got dressed.

Maybe next time, said Craig.

Ray's dad waited for him outside in the car.

You played pretty well tonight, he said.

Could've been better.

It was your first time with a new team. Don't get too down on yourself. Focus on the next game.

Yeah.

They got home. Ray changed and went to sleep.

The school's next game was nine days later, a Saturday. In the meantime Ray's routine didn't change. He went to school, went to practice, helped his dad and hung out with Craig. Sometimes other guys from the team joined in.

He pushed himself in practice. He pushed himself outside of practice. He knew he had to fight for a starting spot, and he'd be damned if he was gonna let some other chump have it.

Ray found his effort overlooked. He didn't start the next game, but he did get about ten minutes in the second half. And he made them count. A twelve point, seven-assist rampage, during which he received a technical for trash-talking someone from the other team. Coach was thrilled. His teammates high-fived him. Craig was impressed.

Good job my man, he said.

Ray smiled at him.

Winter break came around. There were a few practices scheduled for the first week, and an invitation to participate in a city tournament in the second. Ray filled the rest of his time with a chemistry project and hanging out with Craig. They played video games and one-on-one basketball. They talked about life and problems they were having.

Craig invited Ray over one day after a grueling practice. It was the last one before the tourney. Coach made them run suicides for twenty minutes at the end, after over an hour of drills.

I can't feel my legs, said Ray.

He leaned on the counter in Craig's kitchen. His friend was heating up some food. They sat at the table.

I was supposed to take this girl out yesterday, said Craig. But then she started talkin' something about not being ready for a relationship with anyone and I dunno what else, and I'm sittin' over here like, bitch, it's just a date.

Sounds like a pain, said Ray.

Last girl I dated had insecurity problems out the ass, you know, scared I was gonna leave her for someone prettier, always asking me what I'm doing when I'm not with her, that sorta shit.

So what happened?

I left her. She kept begging me to re-think it, saying we were perfect for each other, whatever. I ignored her, man, didn't look back. Haven't dated anyone since.

Ray chuckled.

Can't say I blame you, he said.

Yeah. Oh well. How about you? You got a lady? Anyone you got your eye on?

Uh, nah, not really. Never had a girlfriend, never been on a date or anything.

Really? Damn. I could introduce you to a couple of friends who're single, said Craig. Real nice, smart girls. You'd probably like them.

Hah, thanks man, but I'm good.

Alright, well you wanna go watch something? My parents just bought me Terminator 2, haven't watched it yet.

I've been wantin' to see that, said Ray.

They headed to the basement. Ray sat on the couch as Craig searched for the movie.

I dunno where my parents put anything anymore, said Craig.

He ran upstairs. Ray waited. His friend came back after a couple of minutes.

They would keep it in their room, he said.

He put the tape in the VCR, grabbed the remote, turned off the lights and sat on the couch. He fast-forwarded past the previews.

You ever see the first one?

I saw part of it on TV once, said Craig.

It's good, said Ray, not really an action movie, more of a thriller. The movie started. There were car chases and explosions. Some funny lines and drama. At one point Craig's hand brushed against Ray's. Ray's heart skipped.

Ray eyed Craig's hand again a little later on into the movie. He slowly moved his hand towards it. He brushed Craig's fingers with his own.

What are you doing?

Ray jerked his hand away and turned his head. They watched the rest of the film in silence. Ray couldn't focus. When it ended the two walked upstairs and to the door.

The team's meeting at eight tomorrow right?

Yep.

I'll see you then, said Ray.

Bye.

Ray walked to the bus stop. On the ride home he thought about what happened. He got to the apartment and walked past his father without saying a word. He ate dinner in his room. He went to bed early.

He woke up the next morning and got ready. It was the first day of the tournament. Ray walked to school terrified of how he was going to face Craig. He hoped Craig had forgotten about the movie the day before. He entered the gym. Most of the team was already there. Craig was there. Ray said good morning to Coach and the guys. They greeted him back. Craig didn't say anything. Ray wasn't surprised.

Coach gave the team a talk and told them about the school they were playing and other potential opponents. Then they got on a bus and drove to the civic center downtown.

The place was already filled with the other teams and families and fans. There were eight games scheduled that day. The first game was at nine. Ray's team played at ten-thirty. They watched a bit of the first game and then went to a side court to warm up. Craig still wasn't talking. Not to Ray, at least. Hell, he didn't even look at him. This troubled Ray. His teammates acted normally though. Maybe Craig hadn't said anything to them.

The game was fifteen minutes away. The team huddled.

There's no reason why we shouldn't get through to the next round tomorrow, said Coach. This team's weak in the paint and not particularly quick. Craig, Mike, Teon, Matt, you're starting. Ray, you get in there too. Everybody else, on the bench and watching. You look for mistakes and you fix them when you get on the court.

The boys brought their hands in and did their team shout. They took their places. Ray wondered what was going to happen in the game.

As it turned out, Craig could put aside any personal issues and be professional. The game went smoothly. Ray put in a good performance and the team won by a comfortable margin.

We could've sleepwalked through that, said Coach afterwards. We did well, but that was one of the weaker schools around here. We can't go in tomorrow thinking we'll win because of today. No complacency. Now let's pack it up and go home.

Ray talked with some of the guys on the bus. Craig sat further away and talked to some of the others. They got to school.

I'll see you tomorrow, same time, said Coach.

Everyone got off the bus. Ray walked home. His father was watching television.

How was your game?

Good, said Ray. We're through to the next round tomorrow.

You play well?

Yeah, I'd say so.

I'll try to come down there tomorrow, said Mr. Hamilton. I'll be your good luck charm.

Thanks pops, said Ray.

Mr. Hamilton did make it to the game, though Ray started on the bench. He was thrown in minutes before halftime, played the entirety of the third quarter and was benched again for the fourth. The team trailed in the final thirty seconds and would have lost if not for a last second equalizer from Shakeel to send the game into overtime.

Let's not bullshit ourselves boys, said Coach during the break, we shouldn't be here right now. We ran out of fuel in those last few minutes. Whatever energy you've got, make the best of it. We can book a spot in the final four tomorrow if we hold out for a little bit longer.

They went back out. Ray and Craig started the overtime period together. The team hung in there despite being visibly fatigued. They soon found themselves in the same predicament they were in during regular time, down two points with half-a-minute to go.

They had possession. They brought it up the court. The other school smothered them on defense, and the boys found it hard to get through. Seventeen seconds left.

Craig got the ball. Ray got into an open position and called for a pass. Craig looked at him, then decided to take the shot himself. Bounced off the rim. Opponents got the rebound. Ran. Sunk a three. Buzzer. Game over.

The other team celebrated. Ray put his hands on his hips and looked at the ground. Then he walked to the bench. Coach wasn't too hard on them.

We did what we could, he said. Luck struck once, couldn't get it to strike twice. And that's fine. We hustled and didn't make it easy for them. Don't be too hard on yourselves, we still have the rest of the season and a state championship to play for. I want you all to go home and relax. Don't think about basketball. Be fresh and ready to practice on Monday. Enjoy the rest of your break, guys.

They rode the bus home. Not much was said. They reached the school and disembarked. The players went their separate ways. Craig walked to the bus stop. Ray walked after him.

Hey, he said.

Craig didn't stop.

Hey, Craig.

Craig didn't stop.

Why didn't you pass me the ball? I was open, man. Would've given us a fighting chance.

No acknowledgment. Ray tapped Craig on his shoulder.

Don't touch me, faggot.

This caught Ray off-guard. Hit him right in the gut.

What?

I didn't stutter. I said don't touch me, or I'll beat your little pussy ass.

Craig kept walking. Ray stood and stared at him. Then he walked home, dejected. His father was waiting when he got home.

You look like a sorry mess.

Craig called me a faggot.

Mr. Hamilton was appalled.

Why would he do a thing like that? I thought you were friends.

Cause I did something stupid.

What did you do?

I tried holding his hand during a movie the other day, said Ray. I dunno, I thought maybe, even though he'd been talking about girls right before — I did it anyways.

Did he say anything else?

He threatened to beat me.

His father gave him a stern look.

If he does that again you go straight to the coach, he said. Don't let anyone bully you.

I don't think telling Coach is a good idea, pops. Then all the other guys'll find out.

They're gonna find out anyways.

Ray spent the last days of vacation at home. He went back to school on Monday with a dread-filled stomach. He walked the halls paranoid. He saw some of the guys from the team and they talked to him.

Maybe nothing's wrong, thought Ray. Or they don't know yet.

He sat through his classes and tried not to think about it. The idea of being around Craig at practice intimidated him.

School ended. Ray went to the locker room hoping Craig wouldn't be there. He wasn't. Turns out he was out sick that day. This eased Ray a little, but he still felt tense as he and the team ran through some drills. He went home later that afternoon. All he could think about was whether or not Craig had told anyone.

He'd find out the next day. Classes went without any trouble, and while Craig was still gone, something felt off in the locker room. A couple of odd glances. One of his teammates shoved him on the way to the court. Ray didn't know if it was intentional.

The atmosphere during practice was different from usual. There was an air of apprehensiveness and unease. Nobody said much to Ray, except Coach, who hadn't picked up on the difference in attitudes yet.

Ray got a glimpse of what was to come after practice as the boys showered and changed.

Keep your eyes over there, said Mike. Don't want you getting too excited looking at me fresh out the shower.

I didn't look at you, said Ray.

Mike slammed his locker and walked over. The rest of the team watched.

Craig told me what you did, he said. Warned all of us. So let me tell you, straight-up, you ever try to take a peek at my balls or try to hit on me, or anyone else here, I will bury you.

They glared at each other.

You might be my teammate, but I don't give two shits about you.

I'm not afraid of you, said Ray.

That's cause you're a dumbass. If I were you, I'd quit the team. Go join the cheerleading squad or something.

And you better believe us when we say we'll make sure you stay on the bench, said Matt.

Ray grabbed his bag and left. His fists were still clenched when he got home. His father was making dinner.

You look like you're about to hurt somebody, he said.

Ray walked past him.

What's wrong?

Nothing, he said.

Sure doesn't look like nothing. Something happen at school?

Ray banged his door shut and locked it. He went to sleep.
He contemplated not going to school when he woke up, thought maybe things would tide over while he was gone. He looked in the bathroom mirror and thought about it. Fuck it, if he didn't show up it meant they won.

He was a nervous wreck at school the next day, but he tried to keep his shit together. He saw teammates in the halls and in his classes. As far as they were concerned he didn't exist. Ray thought he heard other people talking about him too. He shrugged it off as best as he could.

Practice was, again, a tense affair, heightened by Craig's presence. Coach noticed this time.

Some of you seem a little uptight, he said. Should cool it a bit before our game tomorrow. Don't wanna play like you've got rods up your asses.

Several of the players snickered. They were still laughing about it in the locker room later.

You hear Coach, Ray? He said he doesn't want you playing like you got something in your ass, said Mike. Best tell your boyfriend to keep it in his pants.

Don't have a boyfriend, said Ray.

Be honest with me, does that hurt? Or is he small enough for you?

Shut your mouth, Mike.

I can't lie to you man, I don't see how you can enjoy that kind of shit.

Without a moment's thought Ray threw Mike against the lockers. The rest of the team gasped. Mike sized him up. Craig stepped in before anything could happen.

Don't bother, he said. If the little bitch wants to think he's tough then let him, won't be long before he gets put in his place.

The team laughed and left the locker room. Only Teon and Ray remained. Teon took a few steps towards Ray. He made sure nobody else was around.

Between you and me, I don't care what you're into, he said. I don't think what they're doing is right.

Thanks, said Ray.

I won't stick up for you though. I'm sorry man, you're a swell guy, but I got my own spot on the team to worry about.

Teon gave him a faint smile and walked out.

Ray spoke to his father at home. He knew he was in the starting line-up for their next game, and he knew Craig and Mike were in it too.

If they want to win, and I can't think of any athlete that doesn't, they'll forget about it, said Mr. Hamilton. They'll work with you, probably reluctantly, but they'll put in the effort. And your coach will know if something's wrong. Just play your game.

Ray kept his dad's words in mind during warm-ups before the game on Thursday. He tried to shake off any jitters he had. He had a bad feeling deep inside.

Not much happened in the first quarter. Both teams played lethargically. Ray knew his performance suffered because he was distracted. It became evident, as the game carried on, that he was an afterthought to his teammates. When he wanted to run a play they were apathetic. When he was open they ignored him. They looked for someone else or forced a shot themselves. Coach benched Ray six minutes before halftime.

The team was losing by double-digits at the break.

We are missing some really easy shots out there, said Coach. We look like we could use some synchronization. And I noticed Ray is hardly getting any looks in his direction. What's the deal?

It was quiet. Someone piped up.

Ray knows why.

Coach turned to Ray. Then he looked at the others.

Whatever the hell it is, he said, you guys had best drop it. We're embarrassing ourselves.

The second half was identical to the first. Ray was an outcast on his own team. At the start of the fourth he asked Coach to sub him out. He sulked on the bench, frustrated with everything about the game. His frustration reached a boiling point when the team magically played better without him. They rallied and won. Coach mentioned Ray again in the post-game talk.

There's some sort of disconnect here, he said, and it's gonna rip us apart if we don't solve it. We won, and that's good, but that's papering over the cracks. Now you can either handle it yourselves like men, or I can get involved. Choice is yours.

You might wanna step in, said Matt. This is a big problem.

Coach talked to the boys separately in his office on Friday. Ray's turn came after a few of the other players had already spoken to Coach. He wasn't sure what to expect.

Hey Ray.

Hey Coach.

How're you doing? Keeping up in school?

Yeah.

Good to hear. You strike me as the type of guy who's always on top of his school work.

Ray nodded. Tension built.

So, uh, listen. I just wanna throw this out there. You're a good kid. You're consistent on the court. This has nothing to do with your performances or attitude.

Alright.

Craig told me. About you-know-what. Said it bothered him a lot. And I can't sit here and say that's the exact truth, but based on what he and a few of the boys said it sounds legitimate, at least to me. They say they don't feel comfortable in the locker room with you around.

Coach I'm not —

I'm not accusing you, Ray. But this is what they're saying. And it's obviously affecting the team.

They're exaggerating it.

They might be. I haven't heard any denials from you though.

Ray sat in silence.

I can't tell you how to live your life. I can't tell you who to like. But I do have a team to look after. That team wants to win a trophy this season. And if there's a hitch on the way to getting that trophy, I need to take care of it.

Why don't you do anything about *them*?

Let's look at this logically. It's a lot easier to risk sitting out one guy than several, don't you think?

Ray knew what was coming.

This won't be permanent. I'd like to have you back, potentially for the playoffs. For the time being, I can't have you near the team. You're welcome to attend our games, of course, we appreciate the support. It could even be good for your development, to sit and watch and take in games.

Ray said nothing.

I understand your frustration, I do. If I was your age I'd wanna be playing too.

Coach extended his hand. Ray shook it.

You know this is horseshit.

I'm sorry, Ray.

Mr. Hamilton was livid when he heard the news. He smashed a plate in the sink and went on a rant.

I'm going to talk to the principal next week, he said. And I'll give him a piece of my damn mind. Can't believe someone in that sort of position would be so prejudiced.

I don't think it's worth the hassle, said Ray. Those kids are gonna give me enough trouble either way. I don't need this blowing up into something huge.

They wanted you to play basketball.

And now they don't. Just let it be, pops.

The hell I will. First thing Monday morning, I'm talking to your principal. And your coach.

I don't wanna transfer again.

You won't.

They dropped the subject for the weekend. Mr. Hamilton tried to get Ray out of the house on Saturday, but he wanted to stay in and listen to *Here, My Dear* on repeat. He did leave on Sunday to go to church, but that was it. He found himself looking in the mirror that evening, reassuring himself he wasn't gonna lose his shit at school, no matter what happened.

Number one, he said, don't respond.

Number two. If you do respond, don't get too caught up in it.

Number three. If you get too caught up, keep your fists down.

Number four. If you get into a fight you make sure you beat the living daylights out of them.

Ray was confident on Monday morning that word had spread beyond the team. He walked into school with his head up, trying to block out everything around him. He reached his locker. He opened it. Inside was a brochure. Ray knew he'd have to deal with taunts and threats that week, but he didn't anticipate it'd come so early.

WHY HOMOSEXUALITY IS A SIN it read. Must have been someone's idea of a joke. Ray crumpled it up and tossed it in a wastebasket as he went to his first class.

Monday went well, about as good as it could have. Mr. Hamilton didn't get his chance with the principal or the coach. The former said he was busy with meetings. The latter refused to cut into practice time to meet with a parent.

We'll try again tomorrow, he said.

Things escalated as the week drew on. In Tuesday's algebra class someone passed him a note with a climaxing penis drawn in it. People cut him in line at lunch. Someone tipped his tray over. He got called a cocksucker.

Same shit on Wednesday and Thursday. Just more of it. Mostly guys, most of whom Ray had never talked to before. Sometimes a girl would jump in and say something like, what's the biggest you've ever had, or, do you spit or swallow?

Through it all Ray gritted his teeth and soaked up the abuse. He had faith that if he ignored it long enough they'd give up and get bored. His father, meanwhile, was having no luck in getting a sit-down with the coach. The principal finally met with him at noon on Friday.

It's really the coach's decision, he said. If he feels like Ray is having a negative impact on the team then there isn't much I can do. But I understand your frustration. If I had a son his age I'd want him to play too.

What about the bullying, Mr. Hamilton said. Ray's told me about the things the students say to him. About some of the things they do. And I haven't heard anything about teachers trying to stop it.

Obviously we can't keep our eyes and ears on every corner of the school. We make every effort to stop bullying. Has he told his teachers about what's going on?

Ray says some of this happens in class, right under the teachers' noses. And they don't care. Don't do a thing.

But has he told them about it?

Of course not. He doesn't think they're any help.

Maybe that's part of the problem, Mr. Hamilton. He needs to tell his teachers, or any adult, what's happening. Then we'll take the appropriate measures.

I'm telling you now.

We'll keep an eye out.

Ok. Thank you for your time.

He went home. Forty minutes wasted.

Ray sat in his history class. He was one class away from freedom for the weekend. There was a basketball game on Saturday. He didn't plan on going, despite being invited by his teammates.

We need an extra cheerleader, said Shakeel. I bet you'd look good in tights.

But make sure you actually cheer, said Matt, and don't get too distracted by the guys on the court.

Last bell of the day rang. Ray flew home.

A brief weekend of solitude and respite.

He returned on Monday. The team won their game, he heard in the halls.

And we did it without you, faggot, said Mike, who'd gone out of his way to pester Ray at his locker.

Leave me alone, said Ray.

How's it feel, knowing we don't need you at all?

Ray slammed his locker shut and socked him in the jaw. That's how it felt to him.

Mike rubbed his face and looked at Ray.

I'm about to rip your skin off, he said. I'm gonna tear your balls off and shove them down your throat. And we'll see how you like that.

I'm not scared of you.

They went at it. A crowd formed. Mike was bigger than Ray, but Ray still landed a few good hits on him. Blood flowed. Two teachers ran over and broke it up. Both were taken to the principal's office.

Go wash your faces off – one at a time – and come back, he said.

Parents were called. Consequences were discussed.

I'm afraid I have no choice but to suspend him, said the principal as met with Ray and his father. We have a no-tolerance policy when it comes to physical aggression.

What about the other boy, said Mr. Hamilton. He provoked Ray.

I've spoken to him and his parents. He says he regrets his actions. We've already given him a suitable punishment.

And that is?

That's none of your concern, sir.

Mr. Hamilton sat bewildered. Ray pulsed with anger.

This could have been avoided, said the principal, if Ray had simply walked away and told a teacher, like I suggested he do. Maybe these next three days will be good for him. He can take some time to cool off and reflect on his actions.

I don't see how this benefits my son at all.

I'm sorry to hear that.

A three-day suspension to start the week. Ray didn't want to go back. His father didn't want him to either. Homeschooling wasn't an option. Mr. Hamilton worked too many hours to be able to do it effectively. Transferring was out of the question.

What are we going to do, Ray, said his father one day.

Don't know. I'm exhausted.

Maybe we can move at the end of the school year. Late summer. I can find a job on the weekend, pull in some extra money.

I could find a part-time job. Help you out a bit.

He paused.

Would you have a problem with me quitting school? For the rest of this year, I mean. I could work some and help get out of here. Do summer school or repeat this year next year. I don't care.

His father thought about it for a few minutes.

I don't see why not, he said. You could learn as much as you would in school, just different skills. Get some work experience under your belt. It's hard to get back into studying and doing homework after you're out for so long.

I know. I'm not worried about that.

Another pause.

I guess I'll go call up the school, said Mr. Hamilton. The sooner the better.

I don't think they'll mind even if we didn't call, said Ray.

Derelict

I woke up one night and looked outside. I saw people climbing out of their windows and into the street. It was two in the morning. I decided to follow them. I walked down my stairs and through the front door.

There were people of all sorts. They all walked the same way. I recognized some of the faces. There was Mrs. Crane, my second grade teacher. Mr. Owen, owner of Martha's Grocery & Gifts. I saw old classmates and neighbors. I saw my dentist and I saw the man from the shoe repair shop down the road. They walked with the most somber of faces. I heard nothing but the sound of feet trudging slowly. Some wore shoes. Some did not. Everyone looked straight ahead of them. The idea of different directions did not exist. They walked.

I joined them. I walked up to Mr. Owen and asked where he was going. He did not answer me. I found a childhood friend and asked what was happening. He did not answer. No one said a word. No one acknowledged me, or anyone else for that matter. They walked.

The city was largely empty. Buildings and homes lit but nobody inside. Twenty-four hour gas stations and restaurants serving nobody. I saw a silhouette here and there, but it always vanished after a few seconds. I saw the occasional car driving off in the distance, but it was always moving away from us. Nobody seemed to notice. Nobody seemed to care. They walked.

I moved against the crowd. I scanned the faces. That's when I saw her. Silky brunette. Wearing her favorite sun dress. Mine too, actually. Like everyone else she walked, unfazed by everything around her. I called her name. And I called again. Didn't look at me. Just walked.

I caught up with her.

What is happening, I said. Where are you going?

I touched her arm.

You remember, don't you, she said. Night-time is unbearable for me. I'm frantic when I'm alone. You never understood that.

Why are you walking?

Loneliness brings desperate measures.

I stopped and looked at all the people walking. Their faces told the same story she told me. People marching into the night searching for a feeling. They walked. I followed.

More voices surfaced.

She's going to take all of my children.

Well I lost a lot of things last year. I feel like I've been through the jaws of hell.

I've been around a few too many times. I've slept with who I want. I don't know if I feel ashamed.

My mother tried to have me locked me up, then she tried to have me put down.

Nobody told me that. I didn't even know.

It wasn't the fact that she turned me down. I just don't like losing. But how can you not feel bad when an ass that fat turns you down?

I spit venom at passers-by.

Do you know what it's like to gaze into total darkness and see the Devil's eyes looking right back at you? Because I do. Every day.

Where are we going anyways.

I followed them for miles. The group approached the city limits. Then we crossed the bridge. They showed no sign of stopping.

We came upon a large hill outside the city. The people moved towards it. They descended towards the forest beyond. The trees swayed with the breeze. The night was tinted with a hue of orange. Clouds gathered.

I stood on the hill and watched people disappear into the woods. Then I heard moans and screams. I heard groans and pleas. She passed by me, walking towards the trees. I didn't stop her. She didn't care. She went in.

It rained. People continued into the forest. Nobody came back out. Yells and cries cracked the sky. A stench filtered through the air. Soon the last person walked in. I was alone.

And I lay my head down on the ground and dreamt.

Gaza Gazali

Naeem was nine years old when his father opened the zoo. It was 1964. The idea came one day when Alia, Naeem's younger sister, was drawing pictures of animals from a book she'd borrowed from a friend. She drew a giraffe and rhinoceros, a toucan and a crocodile.

Baba, she said, I want to see animals like the ones in my book.

And where would you like to see these animals?

Africa! Or the rainforests!

Hmm, said her father, Abou-Naeem. That may be difficult. It would cost a lot of money to travel.

He did not want to disappoint his daughter. A few days later he spoke with some friends about opening a zoo. He would name it The Children's Zoo. The cages would be built by him and his friends. The animals would have to be imported from another country, possibly Egypt or Syria.

Work started immediately. Naeem, though still young, helped his father and the other workers as much as he could. It took them almost two months to finish the zoo. It was small, but a good start. It had a few animals. A couple of horses, some fish, camels, an eagle and a monkey they named Zozo. They also built a swing set. Abou-Naeem was very proud on opening day.

If we take good care of our zoo then you will be its caretaker when you grow older, he told Naeem.

It was the first, and to this day, only, zoo in Gaza. Naeem helped his father after school and on the weekends. Many families visited. The husbands usually sat and drank coffee and smoked cigarettes with Naeem's father. The wives and children walked around and sometimes fed and petted the animals.

When Naeem became a teenager he started working various jobs and saved up money for the zoo. It grew steadily as the years rolled by. During the 70s they brought in another monkey, parrots, ostriches, foxes and a few other types of fish. More importantly, they also brought in two gazelles, which at the time were Alia's favorite kind of animal. Naeem built a slide and a merry-go-round to accompany the swings.

We should add some flowers, or a little garden, said Abou-Naeem one day. It would make this place much more pleasing to the eyes.

It would also help cover the smell of the animals' waste, said Naeem with a sarcastic grin.

His father chuckled.

Maybe I should make you clean their pens more often, he said.

That's a terrible idea.

Hopefully we'll be able to buy a lion soon, said Abou-Naeem. Or a tiger. The kids would enjoy that.

The lion arrived in 1982. Naeem had gotten married and begun working full-time maintaining the zoo with his father. They had grand ideas of adding rides and even more animals.

It could be like a small amusement park, said Abou-Naeem. Imagine that. We could become the most popular place in Gaza.

At the rate the zoo is growing it may actually become Gaza.

Your sister would love that.

Alia would love it if the animals became ordinary citizens with equal rights and freedom to roam the city.

Abou-Naeem laughed.

And then if we have enough animals we could train them to fight the Jews.

I can just imagine the front page of *Haaretz*, said Naeem. Begin assassinated by army of porcupines! Police perplexed!

If only, said his father.

Abou-Naeem found it increasingly harder to work as the decade wore on. He worked only half-days, mostly doing less taxing work like feeding the animals. Naeem himself felt overwhelmed. He had just bought an apartment and his wife was pregnant with a little girl. His sister started teaching at an elementary school. She would bring her class to the zoo at the end of each week if they had behaved and done their work. Abou-Naeem would let them feed some of the animals and sometimes gave the children horse rides.

Naeem's wife gave birth in 1988. They named the baby Khaula.

You know what this means, said Naeem's father that day in the hospital. You get to do everything at the zoo and I can stay at home and spoil my granddaughter. She'll grow up to be a fine young woman.

That's better than my plan. I was going to put her in a cage with the monkeys.

Over my dead body, said Naeem's mother.

The monkeys might do a better job now that I think about it, said Alia.

I can't wait for you to have children, said Naeem.

His daughter was born after the first *Intifada* started, spurred by the killing of four Palestinians by an Israeli army vehicle. Riots and violence broke out. This lasted several years. Thankfully the zoo was not affected, though business slowed. Nevertheless he hired another man to work for him as his father contributed less and less. Alia also got married during this time, to a shop owner in the city.

The zoo nearly tripled in size in the 90s. It added alligators, baboons, hedgehogs and vultures. Naeem also opened a few attractions. A small Ferris wheel, bumper cars and a space shuttle ride. He planned a haunted house. His father was ecstatic.

Naeem's wife gave birth to another child, a son named Kareem, in autumn 1993. Khaula was five years old and attending kindergarten. Alia had a child around this time as well, a boy she named Abdulrahman. Naeem's parents busied themselves babysitting the children.

A new century approached. With it came the second *Intifada*, this one more hostile and brutal than the last. Business again dropped, with the zoo sometimes closed for days at a time as demonstrations erupted across the Palestinian territories. Abou-Naeem would sit and read the newspaper as his son worked.

Did you hear about the soldiers in Ramallah?

No, what happened?

Two Israelis accidentally entered the city and were held by police at the station. Protestors broke in and murdered them.

They murdered them?

Yes. It was a grisly scene. Disemboweled, eyes ripped out. They tossed the bodies through the windows to the crowd outside. Set them on fire and hung them in the city center.

You can only imagine, said Naeem, the sorts of repercussions that will bring.

Israel responded by striking Gaza and the West Bank. Naeem's family, and the zoo, was unharmed, though he wouldn't be so fortunate over the coming years. His mother passed away in 2002. The zoo began to show its age. Repairs and touch-ups waited as supplies and materials were limited. Yasser Arafat, the Palestinians' beloved leader, died in 2004. The *Intifada* ended not long after.

The political party Hamas won a majority in the Palestinian Parliament. Considered a terrorist organization by the West, sanctions were imposed. Financial aid ceased. An economic blockade was placed.

Naeem witnessed stagnation and decline. Fewer families came. The money dwindled. The zoo, bit by bit, grayed. Some animals died. Some were sold off. The garden withered. Rides rusted and broke down. Abou-Naeem's health suffered. After his mother's passing Naeem had tried desperately to convince his father to move in with him. In 2007 his father finally gave in. The house felt cramped. Nobody complained.

See, it's better to be surrounded by family than to be living alone, isn't it, said Naeem's wife.

This is acceptable for now, said Abou-Naeem. I won't be around for much longer as it is. I'll be out of your hair soon enough.

Don't say that, that's morbid, said his granddaughter, Khaula.

Besides, said his grandson, Kareem, if you die the monkeys will be terribly depressed.

You really are your father's son, said Abou-Naeem.

Naeem himself was not growing any younger. Some mornings he woke up and felt pain in his joints. Sometimes during the day he took an extended break while his employees – all three of them, his son included – worked. He still rose at five in the morning every day. On occasion Abou-Naeem would sit at the zoo, mainly out of boredom.

I think I'm going to try to build that haunted house, Naeem said in early 2008.

With what money? said his father.

You could fetch a few shekels. I'm sure there's someone who needs a cranky old man to keep around the house.

I may almost be seventy-nine years old, but I will still beat you with this cane, smart-ass.

Baba, I'd be impressed if you were bothered enough to get out of your chair to chase me.

I'd throw it at you.

You'd never get it back!

They shared a laugh.

I think I can find some cheap lumber, said Naeem. Cut a deal with someone. Find an artist to help me paint it. I'm sure I could finish it by spring, summer at the latest.

You need monsters too. Ghosts and goblins.

That's where you come in.

Eh?

Yes. When the children see your wrinkled face they'll run crying back to their mothers!

Abou-Naeem threw his cane at the back of his son's head.

Construction for the haunted house started a few weeks later. It opened in May. It was designed like a maze. They set up some fake monsters and a small stereo that played a mix of creepy sound effects. When visitors reached a certain point, Kareem, dressed as an evil clown, would chase them. This stopped when an eight-year-old boy became so distressed he cowered on the ground screaming bloody murder.

No more of your antics, said Naeem.

It was your idea, said his son.

Nothing significant happened that summer. Hamas and Israel attempted a truce in June. It lasted until November. The day the United States elected a new president coincided with an Israeli military strike on Hamas. November and December saw more than two hundred rockets fired into Israel.

The Jews are laughable, said Abou-Naeem while reading the news one morning. They want to extend the cease-fire but refuse to end their military activity here.

You wonder how horrible a single country can be, said Kareem.

We don't have to wonder when the evidence is in front of our eyes, said Naeem. We are vermin to them. They'd decimate us if they could. Send us straight to the afterlife.

How ironic for a people to not learn lessons from their own history, said Abou-Naeem.

A few days later, on Christmas Day, Israeli Prime Minister Ehud Olmert appeared on television to give Hamas one last chance to back down.

Do not fool yourselves. We are stronger than you, he said.

It didn't matter. More rockets made their way into Israel that day.

We've survived them before, said Alia's husband that evening during dinner. This time will be no different.

Nearly three-hundred Palestinians were killed on December 27th. Hundreds more were wounded. Among the dead was Naeem's old schoolmate, Bashir. Airstrikes dominated the sky. Naeem was at the zoo, watching his animals panic with every explosion. He worried they would be struck at any moment.

The zoo was spared that day, but many parts of Gaza were not. Government buildings, police stations, mosques and homes lay in ruin.

This is only the first day, said Naeem's wife that night.

More airstrikes came the next day. Israel threatened a ground offensive. Hamas promised the Israelis that Gaza would become a mass grave for their soldiers.

Casualties increased over the next week. Hospitals were unable to cope with the influx of wounded and dying. A ship carrying over three tons of medical supplies was turned away by the Israeli Navy. Humanitarian supplies were delivered by truck at the end of the year. The bombings continued.

Naeem closed the zoo until further notice. He and his workers still worked two hours a day to keep the place in shape. This became a hopeless endeavor. There was little food for the animals. Cages fell apart. Naeem faced a crisis when the zoo lost electricity and water for a week. He and Kareem carried buckets of water from home.

The death toll climbed through January. Each day brought news of someone the family knew.

It will only be a matter of time before they kill us too, said Abou-Naeem. They've made it clear they don't care who they target.

The sight of Israeli soldiers combing through streets and buildings became a daily occurrence. Naeem told his children to keep their distance. If they were approached by a soldier they were to keep their mouths shut.

And Kareem, he said, you will not join the other boys in throwing stones at soldiers and tanks. We do not need to give them more reasons to make our lives miserable.

Alia's school was destroyed towards the middle of the month. The Israelis claimed it was harboring weapons and used by Hamas militants as a hideout. Alia said the only weapons there were the slingshots she took from her students.

But at least we're safe, she said.

The zoo got hit some days later, but not directly. It was early in the morning. A building nearby provided shelter for Hamas soldiers. Israel bombed it. When Naeem arrived for that day's work he nearly collapsed.

Several cages were broken. The animals were too terrified to go anywhere. A few lay dead. Some were wounded. The space shuttle was covered in rocks and rubble. The haunted house was no more.

Naeem went straight to work. The workers and his son joined in. They took a count of which animals were wounded, which were alive, and which were gone. The dead included the lioness, two parrots, a monkey and the alligators. One of the baboons had a gash on her arm. Debris had fallen into the fish pool. Other animals had minor cuts. Some were simply in a state of shock.

This is awful, said Kareem.

It is God's blessing we still have a zoo at all, said Naeem.

It will take a miracle to restore it and fix the rides, said one of the workers. It could take years. How will we get the necessary parts?

The best we can do now, said Naeem, is fix the cages and continue caring for the animals.

We should consider ourselves lucky that nothing happened to the Ferris wheel, said another worker.

They spent that day cleaning. Kareem and a worker brought water for the animals. When the sun set they went home. They repeated this the next day. And the day after.

On January 18th Israel announced a cease-fire. It began pulling out its troops in the evening.

The bastards are only leaving because they want to keep some of us around for the next time they're bored, said Abou-Naeem.

By the twentieth of the month most of the zoo had been cleaned. The cages were fixed, albeit crudely.

That will do, said Naeem. We need to clear the haunted house.

It lay in tatters, unsalvageable. The men figured it would take them the better part of two days to pick up the remains. The men worked for an hour and then stopped to eat lunch.

I will go get some bottles of water, said Kareem. He walked to the small office by the entrance. He entered and found the water. As he left he saw two men walking towards the zoo. They reached the entrance. Kareem ran back to his father.

Baba! Israeli soldiers are here!

Where?

At the front gate.

Did they say anything to you? Did you say anything to them?

No.

Good.

What do you think they want?

I don't know. We'll leave them be.

They ate. They heard the men calling out. Naeem ignored them. They didn't leave.

I'll go take care of this, he said, getting up. They may be looking for someone. Stay here.

He walked to the entrance. The soldiers were standing outside the gate.

Shalom, said one of the soldiers.

We don't want any trouble, said Naeem. There is nothing here but a ruined zoo.

Is this your zoo, sir?

It is.

May we tour it?

This zoo is in no condition for visitors. I suggest you go visit one of your own zoos. Nobody's bombing those.

How much to enter, said the soldier.

Are you deaf? I said nobody is entering this place. Especially not the men who helped destroy it.

Let's go, said the other soldier. This is pointless.

My name is Yossi, said the first soldier. This is Omri. We have been in Gaza —

You've been slaughtering my people.

— for two weeks. We are due to leave tomorrow morning. Would you consider giving us a tour of your zoo? Something to distract our exhausted minds.

Naeem glared at him. The soldier's stance was non-threatening. He spoke broken Arabic. The other soldier did not seem to care as much as Yossi.

Forty-five shekels, said Naeem.

Sir, your sign says twenty-five for adults, said Yossi.

Fifty.

That's ridiculous, said Omri. I am not paying that much.

He left.

Yossi took out some money. He tried to hand it to Naeem, who rejected it.

Put it on that chair, said Naeem.

Yossi set the money down.

You have only ten minutes. You will keep quiet. You will not speak with anyone you see. You will not touch the animals. You will look at the animals and leave. Is that understood?

Yossi nodded. He entered. Naeem returned to his son and the workers. They were waiting for him. They were surprised to see the soldier.

What is he doing here, said Kareem.

He wanted to see the animals. I charged him extra. He won't be here long.

Disgusting. Unfathomable, said a worker. You think additional shekels make up for their monstrosities? The bastard has our blood on his hands. And you let him in. This is traitorous.
Quiet. The sooner he is finished the sooner he leaves. Don't cause a scene.

The worker bit his tongue.

Yossi looked at the baboons. He looked at the camel and looked at the eagle. He looked at the gazelles as well.

These are beautiful creatures, he said. Are they being fed well?

Naeem pretended not to hear him.

What are you feeding them?

Naeem sighed.

Whatever we can find. Rice. We fed bits of the dead animals to the carnivores.

That is disturbing.

You put us here.

The soldier started towards the rides. Naeem followed.

Your time is up. You can't look at those. You need to leave.

Yossi looked at the haunted house wreckage.

What was this?

It was a haunted house. Now go.

The Ferris wheel looks pleasant.

I have asked you twice. I do not tolerate disrespect. Please leave.

The soldier turned and faced him.

As you wish. Have a good day, sir. Thank you for letting me view your zoo.

Naeem said nothing. Yossi left through the entrance and disappeared. Naeem returned to the others. They worked some more and then went home.

Dinner was tense. Kareem, as a naïve fifteen-year-old would, blurted out the day's events. Abou-Naeem nearly suffered a heart attack.

Have you lost your mind! He's probably killed dozens of Palestinians and you let him into the zoo? Are you so weak and motivated by money that you admit a man whose sole intent is to wipe us out?

It's over now, said Naeem. He won't be back.

I'd burn those fifty shekels, said Khaula. It is blood money.

I will do with the money as I please.

Nobody spoke of the incident for the remainder of the night. Naeem and his men returned to cleaning the haunted house mess the next day. Nobody visited.

Naeem was taking a break at noon the day after when a truck pulled up. He immediately recognized the man through the windshield. He stood and waved the truck away.

Go away! Nobody wants you here!

Yossi ignored him. He opened the door and pulled out some large bags. He carried them to the entrance.

Are you not listening, boy? I said leave. Do not bother me again.

The soldier set the bags down.

Your animals are starving, he said. I convinced a friend to donate these bags of food. And I have some medical supplies to help mend their wounds.

Naeem stared in disbelief.

Is there poison in the food? Or are there explosives planted in the bags?

Neither.

What is your motive?

You seem proud of your zoo. It would be a shame to neglect it.

Naeem kept his eyes on Yossi.

Ok, said the soldier. I will leave the bags here. I will not come in. Do whatever you want.

He put them down. He got in his truck and drove off. Kareem came and saw the bags.

What is this, he said.

That Israeli dropped them off here, said Naeem. Said it's food for the animals. And medicine.

Why would he do that?

I don't know.

Are you going to open the bags?

Naeem hesitated.

I suppose, he said.

They went around the animals' cages and fed them. They estimated the bags would last a few days.

The evening at home was tense once more. This time Naeem informed the rest of the family of what happened.

Disgraceful, said his father. I thought you would be stronger. Letting a Jew control you. If anyone from the street finds out they might attack you!

He supplied us with food for the animals, said Naeem. I made him leave. We are not friends.

It will only be a matter of time. He's going to manipulate you.

Yossi did not appear for the next several days. Naeem focused on fixing his rides and attractions. He wanted to rebuild his haunted house.

I don't think we will be able to build it again, said a worker. We do not have the materials. What's left is unusable.

Why does a zoo need a haunted house anyways, said the other worker.

The children enjoyed it, said Naeem. I enjoy running it.

Well perhaps you shouldn't raise your hopes. There's nothing we can do now.

They went home early. Abou-Naeem kept finding something new to lecture or complain about to Naeem every day.

Have you seen him lately, said his father.

No, I think the food was the last of him.

Good riddance. You don't need scum helping you.

The zoo reopened to the public the next day. The rides were closed. The cages were holding up well. There was some food left in the bags. Not many people came.

I imagine it will be like this for a while, said Naeem. No one is going to visit a zoo in these conditions.

Wouldn't leisure be a good distraction, said Kareem.

If you were left homeless would looking at animals be a priority for you?

It wouldn't be.

We ought to be grateful we survived, said Naeem. That we still have our zoo.

A family of five visited late in the afternoon. The little girls and boy were looking at the fish when the truck appeared again.

Oh no, said Naeem.

Yossi was at the front gate. The family saw him.

What is this? Why is this man here, said the father.

I'm sorry. I will tell him to leave.

Naeem ran towards the entrance.

Go away! You're going to scare my customers.

I wanted to ask you a question.

The answer is no.

You don't want to fix the haunted house? I can bring you some lumber.

Naeem gave him a stern look.

Just tell me, he said, what are you getting at? What do you want from me?

I want to help you rebuild your zoo.

You don't know me. And I don't want you to.

I don't need to, said Yossi.

Do you want money? Is Israel not paying you enough? No wonder your people are so foul and greedy.

The family had gathered some feet back and watched the two men argue.

You are not my enemy.

Yes I am, said Naeem. Don't kid yourself. You spent weeks killing hundreds of us.

No you are not. Have you shot any rockets into Israel?

No.

Have you ever maimed Israeli civilians? Damaged our buildings? You have not, said the soldier.

Don't worry, said Naeem, even if I am not your enemy then make no mistake, you are surely mine.

My apologies.

How can you be so calm?

Sir, I am not a murderer, said Yossi. I have not claimed any Palestinian lives. I have wounded some. But I have not killed.

Your association with the Israeli army is enough.

I am serving my country. If you felt your family and friends were in danger I'm sure you'd do the same.

They stared at each other.

Leave, said Naeem. Or I will call the police. And we will make this a much larger problem.

Yossi shook his head and returned to his truck. He drove away. Naeem apologized to the family and went home. Yossi's appearance stressed him enough that his head hurt. That headache nearly turned into an aneurysm when he arrived at the zoo the next morning.

Are you really so thick-skulled? How many times do I need to tell you to leave!

Yossi was standing in front of his truck.

I brought some wood and tools with me, he said. The least you can do is accept it. But I'd like to help.

Naeem eyed him. Then he looked at the things in the truck. He thought about letting the soldier in. It would be an extra helping hand. Naeem did want the haunted house to make a swift return. And Yossi would be able to provide timber and steel poles and whatever else they needed.

He seems polite enough, Naeem thought to himself. And he is willing. I could use him for a day or two and then be rid of him.

Then he looked at the scene around him. Yossi waited for a response. Naeem saw the buildings that had been destroyed over the past month. He saw children running around in the street pretending to be at war, shooting each other with guns made of cardboard. He remembered the friends and acquaintances who'd lost their lives or been injured. His own zoo behind him was crumbling. He took a deep breath.

I'm sorry, said Naeem. You may leave the wood here. But I cannot let you help me.

Silence.

That is fine, said the soldier.

He unloaded the truck. Naeem did not help him. When he finished he walked up to Naeem and extended his hand.

Shalom aleichem, he said.

This caught Naeem by surprise. He looked at the man's hand, then looked at his face.

Walaikum as-salaam, he said, shaking Yossi's hand.

Naeem carried the lumber into the zoo as the soldier drove away. He set it down by the haunted house. He decided not to start that day. He walked home early instead. His family sat in the living room.

The Israeli came again today, he said. He insisted on helping me put the haunted house back together.

Abou-Naeem scoffed.

And what did you do?

I turned him down. But I did take the wood he brought me.

Even that is a step too far, said his father. We can't show that we depend on them for anything.

Yes, I know, said Naeem.

Besides, said Kareem, we built it before. We can build it again. It will be easier this time because we've already done it. I can ask some of my friends to help us.

Tell them we will begin next week, said Naeem. I am going to draw up some plans.

He sat at the kitchen table later with some paper and a pencil. His wife cleaned after dinner. He looked up from his work.

Dear, he said, do you believe everything in life has a purpose? Or has some kind of significance?

Yes, of course, she said. God intends for everything in our lives to have meaning, even if it isn't clear at first. Why?

Because, said Naeem, staring ahead, I can't help but wonder if I just missed an opportunity.

The Adventures of Outlaw Gus and Avocado Duren

It was a beautiful summer day. Two young boys sat behind a table on their cul-de-sac selling lemonade.

This is one of the best days we've had all year, said the boy on the right.

I don't understand why we're not selling anything, said the other boy.

Maybe people aren't thirsty.

Maybe.

The boy on the right, the one with black hair, was Zach Duren. He was known as Avocado Duren. The boy on the left, the bald one with a slight olive tint to his skin, was known as Outlaw Gus. That wasn't his real name, but since Avocado couldn't pronounce that, the name Gus stuck. They were, respectively, the deputy and sheriff of the neighborhood. On most days you could find them riding their bicycles and stopping (minor) crimes. On other days, like today, there would be nothing happening.

It was a very boring day.

I wish Roughneck Randy hadn't gone to camp, said Avocado.

It's a good thing we have a side business, said Outlaw.

The two boys decided to start protecting the neighborhood during the second grade, when Avocado was beaten up on the sidewalk on the way to the park and ended up with a black eye. When Outlaw saw him later that day he laughed. Then he came up with the idea of forming a patrol to make sure no other kids got bullied. And since they liked westerns they decided to be sheriff and deputy. They flipped for it.

I still think you cheated, said Avocado.

I still think you're a whiner forty-niner, said Outlaw.

Gus became Outlaw Gus because it sounded tough. Nobody messes with an outlaw, he had said. Zach became Avocado Duren because, well, no one is sure why. Maybe because the image of an avocado riding a horse made the boys giggle.

The boys had been friends since kindergarten, when Zach moved into the neighborhood. They met because they had gotten in trouble one day for talking during nap-time. And like all best friends they became inseparable, more so than most because they lived right next to each other. It wasn't unusual for one to accompany the other's family when they ran errands. The only times the boys weren't together were the days Outlaw had to go to the hospital and miss school because he was Sick.

So there they sat, trying to make money without a customer in sight. Avocado looked at the lifeless street in front of them while Outlaw played Mario Kart.

Are you ready for school? said Avocado.

I think it's gonna be a good year, said Outlaw. The doctor says things are looking up for me.

Does that mean you won't have to go to the hospital as much?

I dunno, I hope so.

Outlaw kept playing his game. Avocado decided to make a fresh batch of lemonade. A few minutes later they got their first customer, a girl who lived a few houses away. Avocado had a crush on her, though she didn't know it.

Hi Noelle, he said.

She didn't say anything. She handed them a quarter, got her cup of lemonade and walked away.

She's kinda mopey, said Outlaw. Why do you like her again?

Cause her hair looks nice, said Avocado.

The boys took a quick look around and decided to close for the day. They weren't very happy with their earnings.

A quarter for three hours of work. We're gonna go out of business, said Outlaw.

No customers, no crime, this stinks said Avocado.

Good thing school starts in a few days.

Otherwise we'd go crazy being bored.

You got that right.

They picked up the stand and went home. The rest of their summer, as expected, went by slowly. Sometimes they went to the baseball field nearby and played with other kids. Most of the time they sat around their living rooms and watched television or played video games. Or both. One day was a little more exciting though. Roughneck Randy came home from camp and decided to make up for lost time by throwing eggs at people's cars.

The only problem was that he decided to do this at 11:30. On the night before school started. Avocado was asleep when his walkie-talkie went off.

Are you awake, deputy, said Outlaw. We've got a problem.

Avocado opened his eyes and looked at the clock. It wasn't the time to be worrying about any bad guys.

He reached over to his walkie-talkie.

What is it, he said.

Looks like Randy's got a couple of friends over. They're running around causing a ruckus. We need to stop them, said Outlaw.

But I'm tired, said Avocado.

The wicked don't rest and neither do we, deputy.

Can we just call the police?

No.

Avocado rubbed his eyes and sat up. He looked outside. It was a clear night. He looked at Outlaw's house. It was dark. Then he heard something hit his window. He opened it and looked down. There was Outlaw, still in his pajamas. He had a walkie-talkie in one hand and a slingshot in the other. He motioned for his friend to sneak down. Avocado let out a long sigh. He grabbed his badge and his lasso and left the room. He crawled down the stairs and then tip-toed past the living room and kitchen to the back door. He opened it and walked out.

I can't believe we're doing this, said Avocado.

What's the worst that could happen, said Outlaw.

Our butts get kicked and we get grounded.

We could get kidnapped.

That too.

Outlaw pulled out his hand-drawn map of the neighborhood. Ok let's see, he said, they started at Randy's house, made their way over here, and now they're over by Mrs. Fields's house. The good thing is that there are some bushes we can hide in.

It'd be nice if he just gave up, said Avocado.

Outlaw made a face at him.

The boys checked their supplies and started walking. They reached the end of the street when they ran into Randy, which wasn't part of the plan. First they asked him to stop. He said he was innocent. Then his friends grabbed Outlaw and Avocado and held them down. Randy opened his backpack and took out a carton of eggs. The boys squirmed and pleaded but to no avail. Randy egged them both until they were covered in yolk. His friends let them go and they walked off laughing with Roughneck. Outlaw and Avocado looked at each other.

Welp, said Outlaw.

The boys returned home and were promptly grounded until school started.

The school year began much the same as it always did. New people to meet and new things to learn. Outlaw was in Mrs. Leblanc's class, while Avocado had Mr. Mark. The boys met every day for lunch and recess. After school they walked home.

August ended and fall came. The weather cooled and the leaves changed colors. Outlaw and Avocado kept with their homework as well as their neighborhood duty. That was mostly relegated to the weekend since their parents wouldn't let them run around during the week. Outlaw missed his usual days to go to the doctor. Avocado began to notice that his friend would be gone longer than before. When he did come to school he was tired, and when they did their patrols he would wear out easily.

The boys were in Avocado's basement watching cartoons one day in October when Outlaw fell asleep on the couch. Avocado turned the T.V. off and walked upstairs. He found his parents in the kitchen.

Where's Gus, said his father.

He fell asleep, said Avocado.

Maybe you should let him rest for a while, he's been through so much lately, said his mother. Have you noticed?

Yes, said Avocado. He's been gone from school a lot.

I think the doctors have been working very hard to make him better, said his father, and it's taken its toll on him. It's not easy for a kid.

Do you think he's getting better?

Let's hope so.

Avocado sat with his parents and ate a sandwich. His friend soon woke up and came upstairs. They ate together. Then Outlaw walked home.

He continued to miss school, but he did manage to make it to the school Halloween party at the end of the month. Avocado was dressed as a lobster while Outlaw was a ninja. They stood together in the gymnasium and watched other kids play games and dance and drink punch.

Why are you a lobster, said Outlaw.

This was my brother's old costume, said Avocado.

That stinks.

Tell me about it.

You should ask your mom if you can sleep over at my house, said Outlaw. I just got a new game. We can stay up all night and play it.

Ok, said Avocado. But first I'm gonna go ask Noelle to dance with me.

Outlaw stood and watched while Avocado danced - or rather, tried to dance - with the girl. She didn't look like she was enjoying it. He looked like he didn't know what he was doing. He walked back to Outlaw a few minutes later.

I don't think I ever wanna talk to her again, said Avocado.

Their parents came to pick them up at seven. The mothers said it was fine if the boys had a sleepover, but only if they did their homework in the morning. Avocado went home, packed his bag and then went to Outlaw's. There his friend showed him the new game he had bought.

Global Zombie Takeover? My parents would never buy me this, said Avocado.

I promised them I'd wash dishes until I was thirty, said Outlaw.

Avocado read the back of the box.

An open world to explore, over a hundred hours of gameplay, customizable weapons. This sounds like the best game ever.

They bought it for me so I don't get bored when I stay at the hospital.

This caught Avocado by surprise. He looked at Outlaw.

You're going to stay there?

The doctor said I have to. He said I'm not doing as well as I should be.

But that means you won't be at school.

It's ok, my teacher can send me all my work.

And you won't be home.

No, I won't.

The boys sat quietly for several seconds.

Well I'm gonna be dead meat now, said Avocado. Every bully's gonna know it's just me around.

Rule number one, deputy, said Outlaw. Never back down.

If I die you can have my pogo stick.

Ok deal.

The boys laughed and played Global Zombie Takeover. They blasted zombies and saved attractive young women late into the hours. They woke up in the morning and ate pancakes. Then Avocado went home.

Outlaw was admitted to the hospital that Thursday. Avocado didn't see him until a few days later because some relatives had visited from out of town. He finally saw his friend on Monday. When he walked into Outlaw's room he found him watching cartoons with his parents.

Hello Zach, said Outlaw's parents.

Hello, said Avocado.

They brought him a chair. He sat next to the bed and talked to his friend about what had been happening in school. Outlaw told him about his experiences in the hospital. Avocado asked how long he would be there. Outlaw said he didn't know. His mother said hopefully not too long. Then Avocado's parents said they had to go and eat dinner. Everyone said good night.

School changed. When Outlaw was absent in the past everything felt fine because Avocado knew Outlaw would be back soon. Now nobody knew when he would be out of the hospital. Avocado sat alone at lunch most days. Alone for recess too. Sometimes a group of kids would invite him to play dodge ball. He stopped paying attention in class. He was usually busy thinking about seeing Outlaw. His visits so far were restricted to only once or twice a week. One day Avocado asked his parents if they could go to the hospital more often. They said that was fine as long as Outlaw wasn't tired.

Avocado spent Thanksgiving Day in the hospital with Outlaw and his family. They ate turkey and watched football. They played video games and blasted zombies. Avocado left late in the evening. He'd noticed his friend was a little thinner. He asked his parents if that was normal. They said yes.

December greeted the city with a blanket of snow. By now Avocado was visiting Outlaw every day. He would bring comic books and action figures. They would read and play and talk about their plans for when Outlaw got out of the hospital.

I think we should build a fort, said Outlaw one day.

We could put all our stuff in it, said Avocado.

How do you feel about keeping water balloons in there?

What if someone breaks in and steals them?

That would kinda suck.

Maybe we should hide them in a safe, said Avocado.

Where are we gonna get a safe?

I have no idea.

Outlaw laughed. Then they talked about school. Avocado said a boy named Michael kept asking him if he could be the new sheriff. Avocado had to tell him no.

You should make him your assistant, said Outlaw.

I don't think deputies have assistants, said Avocado. You'll be back soon anyways.

I sure hope so.

Avocado told Outlaw he would be gone for winter break. He and his family were going to North Carolina to see his cousins and aunt and uncle. They would be back in January. He asked Outlaw if he wanted anything for Christmas. Outlaw said he didn't celebrate Christmas.

Presents are still nice, said Avocado.

Well, if you insist, said Outlaw.

The trip to North Carolina was both too long and not long enough. Avocado hadn't seen his cousins in a few years, and they had a lot of fun getting to know each other all over again. They played outside and watched movies.

They went to mass together on Christmas Eve. Mr. and Mrs. Duren suggested they say a prayer for Outlaw. The young deputy asked God to help his friend and make him feel better. On Christmas morning they opened presents. Avocado got new socks and a car racing set. He bought Outlaw a cowboy encyclopedia. He wrapped it with a card and put it in his bag.

During the trip Avocado spoke to Outlaw only once on the telephone. He sounded a little tired but was otherwise in good spirits. He told Avocado about all the snow that had fallen.

Maybe we can build a snowman when I get back, said Avocado.

You build, I'll watch, said Outlaw.

The Duren family drove home on the second day of January. They arrived very late at night. Avocado went straight to bed.

School started the next day, which meant there was no time to see Outlaw until the weekend. Avocado was very anxious to give him his gift. He asked his parents if he could skip school one day. They said he could miss half of a day. So on Wednesday, after lunch, Avocado went to the hospital. He had Outlaw's present with him.

When they walked in Outlaw was sleeping. His parents said he'd just fallen asleep.

He's been very tired lately, they said.

Is he getting better, said Mrs. Duren.

We don't think so. The doctors are trying their best.

Avocado set the book on a table.

I bought this for him on my trip, he said. I know you don't celebrate Christmas but I wanted to buy him something.

Thank you, said Outlaw's parents.

The next day at school he asked his teacher, Mr. Mark, if they could make a get-well card for Outlaw. Mr. Mark thought it would be a wonderful idea. The students spent the last period drawing cards. Mr. Mark collected them and gave them to Avocado. He visited the hospital in the evening with his parents. Outlaw was sleeping.

We made cards for Gus today in class, said Avocado.

That's very nice of you, said Outlaw's mother. We can set them over here.

They took the cards and put them next to some flowers. The parents talked while Avocado sat next to the bed.

Mr. Mark said he hopes you get well soon. So does everyone else, he said.

He watched Outlaw breathe in and then breathe out.

I miss you a lot.

Avocado went home. He didn't want to eat dinner. He didn't want to play any games. He curled up in his bed and thought about Outlaw. His father walked in.

Still not hungry?

I don't want to eat anything, said Avocado.

Mr. Duren sat down on the bed.

You know, he said, it says a lot about you that you're this worried about Gus.

I just want him to come back.

I have an idea. Let's take a moment and say a prayer for him. That sound good to you?

Yeah.

Avocado wondered if the Lord was more likely to listen to someone if they prayed extra hard. So he tried. He asked God to make Outlaw healthy soon.

Thank you God. Amen.

Maybe we should do this every day, said his father.

They visited Outlaw again a couple of days later. He was awake this time.

Hey, said Avocado.

Hey, said Outlaw. His voice was quieter than normal.

Did you see your present?

Yeah. It was nice. So were the cards.

I'm glad you liked them.

Is the neighborhood ok?

Not much going on, said Avocado. The other day Jimmy the Jerk tried to put a stink bomb on our doorstep.

What did you do?

I threw it at him.

That's cool, said Outlaw.

He closed his eyes for a minute, then opened them.

Avocado wasn't sure what to say.

So have you beaten the zombie game yet?

Outlaw's eyes were still opening and closing. He mumbled something and drifted off to sleep. Avocado looked on. He felt slightly annoyed. He had come to visit his friend many times and found him asleep on every occasion. He couldn't be too angry though, because he knew Outlaw wasn't doing it on purpose.

Avocado talked with his parents on the drive home.

He isn't leaving for a long time, is he?

Doesn't look like it, does it, said his mother.

No, it doesn't.

The important thing is to keep him in your heart and hope he comes out stronger because of this.

Are you still saying prayers for him, said his father.

Yes I am, said Avocado.

Outlaw passed away a week later. Avocado was at school when he found out. The class was listening to the morning announcements. The principal said that Gus had died very early in the morning. He asked for a moment of silence. The students looked at Avocado. He wanted to run out of the class. He wanted to break things. He wanted to scream at everyone. Instead he found himself stricken with grief. So he stared down at his shoes and cried. First it was a whimper. Then he cried very hard. Mr. Mark came over and hugged him. He said it was ok for Avocado to leave if he wanted. The office called his parents. They picked him up.

We're so sorry, Zach, said his mother.

Just not fair, is it? said his father.

Zach didn't say anything. He got in the car and went home. He went to his room and laid down on his bed. His head hurt. He fell asleep. His mother woke him up a few hours later and asked if he wanted to go next door to see Gus's parents. Zach said no. He just wanted to sleep.

He slept all night. He slept almost all of the next day. When he wasn't asleep he was staring at the wall.

He woke up the next morning. It had been three days already since Gus passed on. He stared at the ceiling and wondered whether he wanted to get up. He tried. His body felt like it weighed a million pounds. So he just lay there.

His father walked in.

How do you feel? he said.

Like dookie, said Zach.

I think that sums it up for all of us.

There was silence.

Did you know they brought Gus home from the hospital?

What do you mean, said Zach.

In his culture it's a custom to bring home the body of the deceased for a day or two before it's buried, said his father. People come and pay their respects.

Zach thought about that.

I don't know if you're ready for it. You haven't left your room. I know it's tough for you.

Do I have to see his face, said Zach.

I think he'll be covered up.

Ok. I think I can go.

He stood up and got dressed. Then he and his parents walked over.

He didn't know what to expect when he walked in the door. He saw a lot of people he didn't know. They spoke in another language. Zach found Gus's parents in the kitchen. He ran straight into their arms and started crying.

There there, said Gus's mother.

He would be very glad that you came, said the father. You're a strong young man.

Where is he, said Zach.

He's in his room. You came at a good time, said the mother. We cleaned his body earlier today. They are taking him to the cemetery in the afternoon.

Zach's parents looked at him.

You don't have to go into the room if you don't want to, said his mother.

He thought about it. He decided it would be better to go. Gus's parents led him to the room. He stepped inside. The first thing he saw was a group of relatives sitting on chairs.

And then Zach saw him. Covered in a white sheet, lying on his bed, was the sheriff of the neighborhood. Suddenly everyone else disappeared. Everything was quiet. Zach stood for what seemed like an eternity. He tried to make sense of what was in front of him. He kept expecting Gus to sit up and say it was all a prank, that he was actually fine.

He waited. And waited. But it didn't happen. Gus lay there, solemn and still. And Zach didn't know what to do, because he was hurt and angry and scared. He didn't move. Then he felt his father's hand on his shoulder.

Maybe you should come sit out here with us, he said.

Zach sat in the living room with the adults. He listened to stories about Gus as a baby. Gus's relatives didn't seem too sad. They seemed happy as they shared memories. One of them asked Zach what his favorite memory of Gus was.

I think it was the time we won a dodge ball tournament at school, he said. There were supposed to be five people on a team, but me and Outlaw thought we could take on everyone by ourselves. It was really hard but we did it. We even got a trophy.

Where did that go anyways, said Gus's father.

I think we traded it to one of the kids at school for two slingshots and a magnifying glass, said Zach.

The adults laughed. Gus's mother served lunch as they talked about other things.

Some men walked in. They spoke with Gus's parents. Then they went back outside.

The hearse is here, said the mother.

Everyone stood up. Zach asked his father what was happening.

I think those are Gus's uncles. They're taking him to the cemetery, he said.

The men came back in with what looked like a stretcher.

We are going to walk into the room and carry Ghassem out, said one of the men to the room. When we come out we do not want to hear any sobbing or mourning! We thank God for life and for his blessings!

They walked in. Zach waited, filled with curiosity and dread. The men emerged a minute later. Gus was on the stretcher, still covered in the sheet. As the men walked through the house Gus's relatives started chanting.

Allahu akbar!

Allahu akbar!

Lah-illaha-il-Allah!

What are they saying, said Zach to his father.

They are saying God is great, he said. And don't you think so, Zach?

The boy sat and watched as Gus was driven away.

Over the next few weeks things went back to normal, or at least as normal as they could. Zach suspended his duties as deputy of the neighborhood. Roughneck Randy stopped by and told Zach he was sorry to hear about Gus. He also said he would stop being a troublemaker until there was another sheriff around.

For a while Zach didn't look for another partner, because he did not want anyone other than Gus. Michael kept pestering him at school, while some other kids he didn't know asked about teaming up with him. Zach rejected them all.

But one day he had an idea. He put up fliers around the block and at school. They said he was looking for a new deputy. He'd promoted himself to sheriff.

He held interviews in his backyard. A lot of his classmates showed up. They were nice, but they weren't what he was looking for. Until he got to the last person, anyway.

Can girls be deputies, said Noelle.

Yes, they can, said Zach.

हरे कृष्ण

Hare Krishna

हरे कृष्ण

Hare Krishna

कृष्ण कृष्ण

Krishna Krishna

हरे हरे

Hare Hare

हरे राम

Hare Rama

हरे राम

Hare Rama

राम राम

Rama Rama

हरे हरे

Hare Hare

Acknowledgments

Here's to Mrs. Pippen, Mrs. Gillogly, Mrs. Ferguson and Mrs. Miller, my elementary school teachers, for teaching me how to write.

Shout-out to Mr. Ingles, Mrs. Waibel, Mrs. Applen and Ms. Mellies, my middle school English teachers, for encouraging me to keep writing.

To my high school English teachers, Ms. Lane, Mrs. Strong, Mrs. Powell and Mr. Anderson, who helped me refine my writing. Thank you to Dr. Kerns for letting me write for the high school paper all four years.

Huge props to Ann Sargent and Ron Holohan, my composition professors, for showing up at exactly the right moment in my life.

To Frank Radosevich, Lisa Miller and Dr. Netzley for teaching me the ways of writing like a journalist.

A big thank you to Tanya Koonce and Denise Molina for a very educational six months at WCBU.

To Dr. Burgauer, Dr. Swafford, Dr. Katz, Dr. Glassmeyer, Dr. Palakeel, Dr. Conley, Dr. Muzzillo and Dr. Craig, my English professors at Bradley.

A token of great appreciation to the following people, whose tremendous generosity helped make this book a reality:

Adam Amrani
Adriana Pabon
Aleksey Lykov
Alicia Kelly
Brett Davis
Craig Auker
Doug Tucker
Eric Eagan
Erik Johnson
Hayley Brewer
Jase Chun
Jason Castle
Joshua Kovarik
Kaylee Webster
Khaula Abou-Hanna
Kiran Balan
Maxwell Riley
Maxwell Sowell
Melissa Del Rio
Mohammed & Alia Shanaa
Mona El-Sawaf
Ned Swanson
Ryan Coyne
Sarah Rayfield
Seth Kasky
Thanand Kachentawa
Todd Jelken

Music

This is a complete list of all the music I listened to during the creation of this book.

Andy Stott - Luxury Problems
Burial - Untrue
CFCF - Exercises
Clams Casino - Instrumental Mixtape 2
Daughn Gibson - All Hell
Death Grips - The Money Store
Deftones - Koi No Yokan
DJ Shadow - Endtroducing...
Fenessz - AUN
Flying Lotus - Until the Quiet Comes
Flume - Flume
Fugazi - The Argument
Gaza - No Absolutes in Human Suffering
Gil Scott-Heron - I'm New Here
Godspeed You! Black Emperor - 'Allelujah! Don't Bend! Ascend!

Godspeed You! Black Emperor - F#A#∞
Godspeed You! Black Emperor - Lift Your Skinny Fists Like
Antennas to Heaven
Halls - Ark
Hüsker Dü - Zen Arcade
James Blake - James Blake
Johann Johannsson - Copenhagen Dreams
Kendrick Lamar - Good Kid, M.A.A.D. City
Kevin Drumm - Relief
Kid606 - Lost in the Game
Kid606 - P.S. I Love You
Liars - Drum's Not Dead
Liars - Sisterworld
Liars - They Were Wrong, So We Drowned
Lust for Youth - Growing Seeds
Martin Stig Andersen - Limbo (Original soundtrack)
Michiru Oshima & Pyramid - ICO: Melody in the Mist
Mogwai - Happy Songs for Happy People
Mogwai - Young Team
My Bloody Valentine - Loveless
My Bloody Valentine - m b v
Neil Young - Le Noise
Nick Drake - Pink Moon
Nine Inch Nails - Broken
Raime - Quarter Turns Over a Living Line
Shabazz Palaces - Black Up
Shackleton - Music for the Quiet Hour
Taken by Trees - East of Eden
Tim Hecker - Dropped Pianos
Tim Hecker - Radio Amor
Tom Waits - Alice
Tom Waits - Bone Machine
Tricky - Pre-Millenium Tension
Zaturn Valley - aether

ABOUT THE AUTHOR

Wassim Elhouar is a writer from Peoria, Illinois. He published his first book, *I Know What I Know Now*, in January 2011. He is also the founder and owner of Midnight City Press, a publishing house dedicated to releasing works by independent authors and poets.